CONFRO

A NOVEL

Mohamed Latiff Mohamed

Translated from the Malay
by Shaffiq Selamat

EPIGRAM BOOKS
SINGAPORE · LONDON

Epigram Books UK
First published in 2013 by Epigram Books Singapore
This Edition published in Great Britain in January 2019
by Epigram Books UK

Copyright © 2019 by Mohamed Latiff Mohamed
Translation copyright © 2019 by Shaffiq Selamat
Cover design by Stephanie Wong

The moral right of the author has been asserted.

**A CIP CATALOGUE RECORD FOR THIS BOOK IS
AVAILABLE FROM THE BRITISH LIBRARY.**

ISBN 978-1-912098-57-6

PRINTED AND BOUND IN
Great Britain by Clays Ltd, Elcograf S.p.A.

Epigram Books UK
55 Baker Street
London, W1U 7EU

10 9 8 7 6 5 4 3 2 1

www.epigrambooks.uk

To my faithful wife, Jamaliah Md Noor,
my sons, Khairil and Haikel,
my beloved granddaughter, Batrisyia Noor Tasneem,
and my loyal friends in Asas '50.

CONTENTS

CAST OF CHARACTERS

Adi	A young village boy
Mak Timah	Adi's mother
Pak Mat	Adi's father
Ani	Adi's older sister
Omar	Ani's husband
Pungut	Adi's adopted sister, Busuk's biological daughter
Abang Dolah	The village bomoh and a political activist
Kak Habsah	Abang Dolah's lover and common-law wife
Bibik	Elderly Peranakan woman who raises ducks
Busuk	Bibik's daughter and Pungut's biological mother
Ah Kong	Chap ji kee towkay
Tong Samboo	Chinese mother of two children, a boy and a girl
Tong San	Seventy-year-old Chinese man
Kak Salmah	Violent woman with a gold tooth, samshu addict
Jamilah	Kak Salmah's adopted daughter
Bongkok	Shop owner, sells samshu illegally
Pak Abas	Richest man in the village
Bibi	Divorcée with three children, seduces the village's married men
Adi's friends	Kassim Boca, Yunos Potek, Dolah Supik, Yahya, Sairi, Basri
Assorted villagers	Yusoff Gemuk, Mail Sengau, Daud Cina, Mama Sulaiman, Ali Spring

PART

1

ANI DISAPPEARS

THE ENORMOUS BANYAN tree in the centre of Kampung Pak Buyung, one of Singapore's many rural villages, had always been a topic of conversation for the people who lived around it. Mandarin oranges and joss sticks had been inserted in the crevices between its roots. Some of the joss sticks, precisely six, had burnt out. Soon, the Mandarin oranges too would disappear—left there as offerings by the Chinese villagers, they were often eaten by famished children. The banyan tree was already said to be several hundred years old; it was also said to be haunted, and no one dared to walk under it after dark. Its branches were the girth of an embrace. Its majestic canopy of leaves gave shade to the attap-roofed houses beneath it. Its roots were each the size of a man's arm. The trunk of the banyan was thick and bore many incision marks; many bird poachers had come and cut the tree for its sap, which would then be mixed with vinegar and used to trap birds.

The giant of a tree was a playground for Adi, who would swing from it like Tarzan. He would climb up and gaze at the far-off Cathay Building from his perch. He would look down at the cauldron-sized holes formed by the tree's intersecting roots, far below. Rumour was that, once in a while, two or three monitor lizards would come out of these holes, raise their heads, and then turn around with a flourish to once again hide themselves under the roots of the tree. Adi had never come face to face with these "spirits" of the banyan tree, but whenever he thought about them, he always remembered Abang Dolah's story about the hantu jerangkung, the skeleton ghost. Abang Dolah often told this story on Friday nights, when Adi pressed him for ghost tales. The skeleton ghost, the story went, would appear around evening, and then wander about the latrine tanks. That was why, Abang Dolah said, if the skeleton was present around dusk, the whole village would stink of shit.

Adi tried to look down the length of the banyan tree, but could only see its hanging roots, which were gnarled and twisted. Adi would use these arm-thick roots to slide quickly down the tree. His mother would shriek whenever she saw him clinging to the banyan roots, terrified that he would fall. She believed that the banyan tree always claimed victims. That was why the Chinese people in the kampung made offerings to the banyan tree.

• • •

One day, Adi climbed down the tree to find two men crouched at its foot, shaking for numbers. They were trying their luck at chap ji kee, a game of chance and illegal lottery.

"Go away, go away!" one of the men shouted. He wore a torn singlet, and shooed Adi off.

"Sa, ji, kau," Adi teased the man as he left, reciting

Hokkien numbers he had no intention of betting on, his eyes focused on the Mandarin oranges below. He intended to take them once the Chinese men were gone. Adi walked home. He sat on the ambin, a low wooden platform on the veranda in front of his house, staring at the banyan tree. He thought about the lizards, the spirits of the tree. Hundreds of starlings flew about and then perched on its branches.

Adi felt the beginnings of hunger pangs. Since afternoon he had only eaten two guavas, stolen from behind Bibik's house. Usually, if there was any rice left over at home, his mother would ask him to give it to Bibik, who would then feed it to her ducks. For the past few days, though, his mother had not asked him to deliver any leftover rice to Bibik. This afternoon, while wandering in the banana plantation behind Bibik's house, Adi had seen two yellowing guavas. He had climbed the guava tree stealthily, afraid that Bibik would hear him. She would normally curse at him if she saw him climb her guava tree.

Bibik actually did not care so much about her guavas, which after all, no one ever ate. When they ripened, they just fell and were squashed on the slushy ground, right where her ducks soaked themselves in the mud. Adi would often pick up the guavas that had fallen to the ground, wash them at the well, and eat them later. This time though, Adi had plucked the two half-ripe guavas off the tree and then quickly fled into the banana plantation to eat them.

Thinking still of the guavas, Adi got down from the ambin, walked into the house, and entered the kitchen.

His mother was cleaning some tamban fish.

"Go fetch some water," she said. "Your father will want to have a bath when he comes home. There's no more water." Adi suddenly thought of a story Abang Dolah had told him, about the pontianak, a vampiric female ghost that preys on men; he'd said that if a pontianak cleaned fish with her hands, she would eat up every bit of the fish's stomach.

Adi reluctantly picked up a bucket and two empty kerosene tins. The well was located about twenty metres from his house; the water in it was clear. About ten families used this well; among them were Adi's family, Ah Kong the chap ji kee towkay (or boss), Tong Samboo and her two children, the Chinese coconut-husk peeler (who had five children, one of them with a pink face), Abang Dolah, Mama Sulaiman and his son Ali, and Tong San the seventy-year-old Chinese man whose wife nevertheless gave birth to a baby every year (Adi's mother had said that whenever Tong San's wife delivered a child, he himself acted as the midwife).

Adi made his way to the well, passing by Tong San's house. Inside, Tong San's wife was cleaning some pork, and her most recent baby was sleeping, strapped to her back with a red sash; Adi found the smell of the pork unpleasant. Her other children were roaming around nearby, playing in a drain, catching worms. As Adi walked past Abang Dolah's house, he noticed that the door was locked, concluding that Abang Dolah was probably not at home.

The area around the well was partitioned using rusty metal hoardings. It was divided into two parts, one section which allowed privacy for the women to bathe. The floor around the well was mouldy and slippery, and the bricks of its walls were broken and eroded, covered with layers of moss. Adi lowered his bucket inside; the water level had gone down. A small sepat fish was swimming inside, and a fallen hibiscus flower floated on the water's surface. Adi drew up his bucket and emptied the water into his kerosene tins.

Whenever someone accidentally dropped their bucket into the well, Adi would volunteer to climb down to retrieve it, using the bricks set into the walls of the well as handholds. For this effort, he would get ten cents. Adi had become adept at this retrieval, and was always called upon whenever someone lost a bucket. Except, of course, for the coconut-husk peeler; he had a pole with a hook attached to it, so if his bucket fell into the well, he would pull it out himself.

After both the kerosene tins were full, Adi carried them back. By the time he reached home, his mother had finished cleaning the fish. Adi's father had not yet returned home. He worked near Kallang Airport, where he kept watch over dredger vessels that were being repaired. He often came home late at night, or sometimes, not at all. One time, he had found his father gambling two days after his payday.

"Where's Ani?" his mother asked, a few strands of her greying hair having fallen onto her cheeks. "I've not seen her face since morning. Go look for your sister after you finish with the water. No shame! A girl like her shouldn't be loafing at others' houses."

Adi made another trip to the well, this time to fill up the earthenware jar used to store water in the house. When he started to draw up his bucket, he heard somebody from the other side of the well area, where the women bathed. When he lowered down his bucket again, he saw a fair hand doing the same; Adi guessed it was the coconut-husk peeler's daughter. She was a beautiful young woman with rosy cheeks and a voluptuous body. Their buckets knocked against each other and Adi felt a thrill. Abang Dolah, whose house was quite close to the well, would often peep at her whenever she took a bath; he would then giggle and run back into his house.

After three rounds of walking back and forth, carrying the two kerosene tins of water each time, Adi had filled the earthenware jar. Adi then noticed that the other jar, the one used to store drinking water, was half-empty. Later, he would have to fetch water from the communal tap, which was located about one hundred yards from Adi's house; if not, his mother would certainly nag him. Adi resigned himself to the long queue that he would have to join in order to complete his chore.

His mother was frying the tamban fish she'd been preparing, and Adi found the aroma stimulating. She gave

7

him the smallest piece. Munching on the hot tamban fish, he stepped out of the house and set off towards Kak Salmah's house, in search of his sister.

The day was turning to dusk, and the leaves of the banyan tree had begun to darken. The coconut-husk peeler was eating porridge on his veranda. His son, the one whose face was pink, was not eating, but was still peeling the husks off some coconuts; Adi found the sour smell of the husks unpleasant. He took a shortcut, passing by a row of barrack houses whose residents were all Chinese. The kitchens of these barrack houses were located towards the front, and the aroma of Chinese cooking also bothered Adi as he walked past. Between the kitchens and the footpath ran a drain, which was full of scattered garbage. On reaching the end of the row, Adi turned towards Kak Salmah's house. Old bicycles had been left leaning against the walls, here and there.

Adi found Kak Salmah eating, along with her adopted daughter Jamilah. Kak Salmah used chopsticks instead of her fingers, like a Chinese person. When she saw Adi, she invited him to join her, but he declined. He looked inside Kak Salmah's house for Ani, but his sister was not there.

Kak Salmah was pretty, her skin tanned and attractive. Her shoulder-length hair hung loose, and her body was slim but curvaceous. One of her front teeth was set with gold, and when she smiled, her gold-inlaid tooth gleamed. Some people said she worked as a hostess in a bar at Lorong 25. Others said she was a hustler. Adi had noticed that

Kak Salmah often changed partners: some were Eurasian, some Chinese, some Indian, but never Malay. Kak Salmah was on familiar terms with all her Chinese neighbours; she was fluent in Mandarin and could speak various dialects, including Hainanese, Hokkien and Cantonese. She was also a fierce woman when she got drunk on samshu; she would beat Jamilah until the girl was half-dead, and Jamilah's face was perpetually disfigured as a result: her lips swollen, the skin around her eyes blue-black, her face covered with scars.

"Please get me some samshu from Bongkok's shop," Kak Salmah said to Adi, handing him a fifty-cent coin and an empty gripe-water bottle. "Buy thirty cents' worth. You can keep the twenty cents change."

Adi immediately darted to Bongkok's shop, which was located about one hundred yards from Kak Salmah's house. The dilapidated old store was sheltered under a cotton tree. Bongkok had opened his shop in the middle of Lorong 23 decades ago, and he sold samshu and lottery tickets illegally, something which had gotten him arrested many times. He would only entertain people whom he knew, and often went about his business without putting on a shirt. His breasts sagged because of old age, and his body had become flabby.

"Bongkok, give me thirty cents' worth of samshu," Adi said, handing over the gripe water bottle and fifty-cent coin.

"For whom?" asked Bongkok, warily.

"Kak Salmah, Salmah lah!"

Bongkok went into another room. He drew the curtain over the door and disappeared. Adi's eyes roamed around Bongkok's shop. The wooden walls were very old, ugly, and black. A Chinese deity figurine stared intimidatingly at him from an altar; two candles and three Mandarin oranges had been placed as offerings at its feet. Sacks of sugar, rice, flour, salted fish, dried melon seeds and dried squid lined the walls, along with Chinese prayer candles and several tins of biscuits. The floor of the shop was uneven dark mud, as though distended by tiny, pitch-black anthills.

Bongkok soon returned with the gripe water bottle, now full of samshu. His mouth also reeked of the drink. Adi took the bottle and the twenty cents change, and immediately left for Kak Salmah's house. He tried to smell the cork. The samshu's sharp odour seemed to sting his brain.

Upon reaching Kak Salmah's house, Adi was shocked to see her pressing Jamilah's face into the dirty cement floor of her house. Jamilah was shouting and crying. She struggled and asked to be let go. Her nose was bleeding.

"You swine! Damned child! Can't even eat properly, so messy. I slut around to feed her! Damn it! I'll kill you!"

Adi handed over the bottle, and Kak Salmah snatched it with the expression of an angry lioness. He hurriedly left the scene, the coins clinking in his pocket. As he walked away, he could still hear Kak Salmah swearing at Jamilah.

Adi walked past some Chinese houses and reached the kolong of Pak Abas's house, dimly lit by a gloomy street lamp. Pak Abas was the richest man in the village. He had constructed about twenty barrack houses, which he rented out to satay sellers, mee rebus sellers, and taxi drivers from Malacca. The kolong of Pak Abas's house consisted of loose soil; this space under the stilt-raised kumpung house was where Adi usually played with his friends. Adi looked around for Kassim Boca, Yunos Potek or Dolah Supik, but none were there yet. Adi continued wandering around. He peeped through the slit in a wall of the nearby surau and saw two rows of people performing their prayers within the hall. He left and headed for a sarabat stall by the roadside at the junction with Aljunied Road. This was the regular hangout for residents of Kampung Pak Buyung. They would play poker, eat prata, tease passers-by, and discuss politics here.

Adi saw Dolah Supik coming towards him on his bicycle. Dolah Supik saw him too.

"Would you like to watch a ten-cent movie?" asked Dolah Supik rather politely. "*Sumpah Orang Minyak* is playing at Jalan Alsagoff tonight."

"Give me a ride!" Adi shouted. The twenty cents he now had was enough: ten cents for the movie, five cents for turnips (which he would eat with petis, a delicious congealed fish paste), and five cents left over to buy opak, which were fried cassava chips. As he thought about the movie and the snacks, he forgot about his sister.

The bicycle had big mudguards. Adi rode pillion, while Dolah Supik pedalled. They used a shortcut to avoid being spotted by a policeman, since riding pillion on a bicycle was a chargeable offence. They rode through Lorong 25, then through Lorong 29, and came out at Kampung Wak Tanjung. Then they entered Jalan Afifi, passed by a sewage processing plant, and entered the Kampung Paya area. Dolah Supik was short of breath.

There were drains on both sides of Jalan Denai, with tall shrubs here and there. The narrow ground was uneven; Dolah Supik lost control of the bicycle a few times, and it very nearly went into a drain, so Adi had to climb down and help push the bicycle. He got back on again when the road was smooth.

• • •

The area where the ten-cent movie was to be shown at Jalan Alsagoff was brightly lit. To the right of the open-air stage was a Chinese temple, in front of which were many hawkers. He and Dolah Supik bought some opak and petis-mixed turnip from an Indian man, then Dolah Supik took Adi's ten cents and bought both their movie tickets. Adi munched on his spicy turnip, and the petis and chilli sauce abruptly seared the inside of his mouth and throat. He wanted to buy some water but had no more money. Dolah Supik kindly lent him five cents, and Adi immediately gulped down a cup of sugarcane juice.

That night, Adi watched *Sumpah Orang Minyak (The Curse of the Oily Man)* with rapt attention. His mother's instructions to look for his sister, who had not come home all day, were gone completely from his mind.

WHICH PARTY WILL YOU VOTE FOR?

IT WAS LATE at night by the time Dolah Supik dropped Adi off. The light from the pressure lamp at the sarabat stall had begun to dim and the canvas blind had been lowered. The surau was already dark and quiet. To reach home, Adi would have to face packs of dogs; he looked around for a good-sized stick that he could use to ward them off. Gripping firmly on to a small wooden stick he found nearby, he walked past the satay sellers' barrack houses. Adi noticed that many of them were still awake and busy preparing satay by skewering pieces of meat onto thin sticks. He had to walk carefully because the cement flooring was slippery.

In the clearing in front a Chinese temple, there stood a large angsana tree, the full moon clearly visible through its leaves. This area had the most dogs that Adi knew of; several of the mangy animals glanced at him, and a few bared their teeth. He held tight onto his wooden stick and waved it to frighten them off. He continued walking. As he passed Kak Salmah's house, he noticed the door was still open; Kak Salmah sat inside, facing a dark-skinned man, both of them munching on fried peanuts. Three empty bottles of stout were on the table.

Finally home, outside the house, Adi could see a kerosene lamp burning brightly inside, and his parents on the ambin, talking to Abang Dolah and Bibik. When Adi stepped through the door, his mother glared at him; his father, however, remained intent on his Poker cigarette. Abang Dolah scratched at the white spots that constantly plagued his neck. He was a lean man, and his spectacles and broad forehead gave him a scholarly look, which may well have been merited—it was generally said that Abang Dolah had passed his Senior Cambridge Examinations, he could speak and write English quite well, and he was good at teaching children to recite the Quran. Though he had at one time worked as a clerk, Abang Dolah did not like to hold a salaried job. Currently, he was on welfare and received thirty dollars every month.

Adi's sister Ani was sleeping on a mengkuang mat, on the floor; she looked completely exhausted and had fallen into a deep sleep. Adi's gaze then turned to a big lizard on the wall, next to one of the holes through which Adi would sometimes peep to spy on his next-door neighbour, Ah Kong, who often smoked opium. It was not unusual to see two or three people sprawled on the floor of Ah Kong's house, the sound of a classic Chinese song from his Rediffusion radio filling the air. Adi had been inside Ah Kong's house several times, conveying Abang Dolah's chap ji kee numbers; Ah Kong would stay inside his yellowed mosquito net, the room ripe with a foul odour mixed with the lingering tinge of Tiger Balm. To the left of his bed was a China-made spittoon with an engraved design of flowers.

Adi turned his attention to Bibik's conversation with his mother.

"A curse on Busuk. Rotten girl. She doesn't want to look after her own child. Do take it, Timah, please!" Bibik wore a batik sarong with a kebaya, an outfit typical of her Straits Chinese culture, and was chewing on some quicklime-coated betel leaves. Like Adi's mother, her hair was grey, although she was much older.

"I don't know," said Mak Timah. "Let me sleep on it."

"Please take it. We will pay for its birth certificate and letter of oath. Busuk will give you another two hundred and fifty dollars," Bibik said, adding, "Damn Busuk! She went to see a datuk; the high priest said the child would bring bad luck! No one else wants to take care of it!"

Adi's mother remained silent.

Bibik continued: "If no one wants the child, she will abandon it. Her heart is rotten."

"Let me consider it, Bibik," Adi's mother replied. "At this age, I'm not keen to look after a small child."

"Let me look after Busuk's child, Bibik," Abang Dolah interjected, puffing away at his Poker cigarette. The smoke filled the room.

"You want to look after a child?" Bibik said, sucking her few teeth loudly. "Your own kitten is undernourished. Your welfare money is not enough for you to buy cigarettes. Yet you have the cheek to say you'll look after a child!"

She paused for a moment and her shoulders slumped. "I have to go home. Busuk and her husband have gone to watch wayang pek ji, the Chinese opera near Lorong 3. There's no one at home. I should leave now." She adjusted her fading batik sarong and left, disappearing past the dim light of the street lamp in front of the coconut-husk peeler's house.

"Auntie, Uncle," Abang Dolah said to Adi's parents, changing the subject abruptly, "on polling day, who do you plan to vote for?"

"I don't know. Anyone will do," Adi's mother casually replied.

"Vote for the goat's head logo party, Auntie. That's the people's party. Our own people. If they win, they'll be able to help the people."

"What kind of help?" said Adi's mother. "Can they give us money? Can they replace the leaking roof of my house?"

It was now getting late. The faint melancholic sound of classic Chinese songs from Ah Kong's radio could still be heard. Adi began to feel drowsy. Through his sleepy haze, he could still hear Abang Dolah trying to convince his parents to vote for the party with the goat's head logo.

Adi fell asleep to the sound of their voices.

COLONISERS ARE DOGS

ABANG DOLAH wore a yellowed singlet that had once been white and his thick pair of spectacles, and was playing "Sri Mersing", a classic Malay song, on his violin. He was a member of Norjawan, and his band was often invited to play at weddings. His house was very small. He had made an ambin from the wood of some discarded milk cartons; a mengkuang mat and several pillows were placed on it. The white pillowcases over them had also turned yellowish and were stained with saliva. Next to the ambin was a milk carton, placed on top of a sheet of newspaper, along with a mug and two glasses. There was no kitchen.

Abang Dolah was a bomoh, a witch doctor. He had quite a number of clients and knew how to cast black magic; he also knew how to make love potions, hate potions, and other such concoctions. He was divorced; his son, Zainal, lived with his ex-wife, who was said to have come from a rich family.

As Adi came into the house, Abang Dolah stopped playing his violin. He stood up and reached for the pair of trousers that hung on a hook on the floral-wallpapered wall. Reaching into a pocket, he took out a coin and a matchbox.

"Adi, go and find me some worms from a carcass. Any

carcass will do. Take three or four worms and put them in this matchbox."

He then handed Adi the twenty-cent coin. Adi had no idea what Abang Dolah wanted the worms for, but he supposed that Abang Dolah would use it to make some medicine.

Adi walked past Bibik's house. He saw Busuk sweeping the floor. She was around thirty years old, Bibik's eldest child, and she always wore a cheongsam with a high collar. Busuk could not speak Malay well despite the fact that Bibik was a Peranakan and therefore, by all rights, should speak Malay as her mother tongue.

Adi headed straight to the river near Lorong 17. He often saw the dead bodies of various animals there, with cat carcasses being the most common. Adi reached the smelly riverbank and noticed lots of flies around a log that lay next to some strewn garbage. He was lucky, for indeed there was a cat carcass there. The cat's stomach had been burnt, and big, fat worms were squirming all over the gaping wound. Adi picked up a satay stick from the ground and held his breath against the strong stench. He felt like vomiting, but managed not to. He poked at the worms on the swollen carcass with the satay stick, and pushed them off the dead cat and into the matchbox. He then closed the matchbox, put it in his pocket and walked quickly back to Abang Dolah's house.

As Adi reached Abang Dolah's house, he could hear the bomoh still playing his violin. He also noticed a pair of ladies' slippers outside the door. Adi went inside to find Kak Habsah sitting on the ambin, and a metal tiffin balanced on the milk container.

Kak Habsah was in her early thirties, with a plump body and a round radiant face. She worked as a domestic helper in Siglap and lived in Lorong 21. Adi had heard from his mother that Abang Dolah kept Kak Habsah (who in fact was married to someone else) as his mistress. As Adi entered, Kak Habsah stepped out, saying that she was leaving for work.

Adi handed over the matchbox with the worms to Abang Dolah. He took a quick peek inside before closing the box and placing it on the ambin. He then stood up, put on a white short-sleeved shirt, and combed his hair, which he always kept neat.

"Some members of the People's Party will be giving a talk today," he said. "I shall leave now."

In response, Adi stepped out of the house. Abang Dolah followed, locking the door with a small padlock.

• • •

Adi headed towards the well to check if anyone had dropped his or her bucket. He saw some tiny sepat fish come up near the surface of the water before diving back down again. Adi plucked two nearby stalks of hibiscus flowers and threw one into the well. The flowers swayed as the water rippled out to the edges of the well's walls. Adi felt the sudden urge to go to the People's Party rally. He walked to his house and peered into the bathroom, where he saw his mother doing the laundry. His sister was nowhere to be seen, and his father was also not around. Usually, on Sundays such as this, his father would go out early in the morning to the sarabat stall; he would sit there all day, playing poker, and would only return home late at night.

Adi made his way to the kolong of Pak Abas's house, where he found Dolah Supik, Yunos Potek, and Kassim Boca. They were sitting around, munching on rose apples. Opposite Pak Abas's house was normally a plot of vacant land, but on that day a tent decorated with coconut leaves had been put up there, complete with around a hundred chairs and a stage on which stood a microphone, with many people milling about. They all were dressed in baju kurung and songkok, the traditional Malay suit and headdress, and wore the badge of the party that had the image of a goat with horns for its logo. The residents of Kampung Pak Buyung had already taken up half the seats. Adi saw his father sitting in the first row, recognising his songkok very well; it was worn-out and rode high. Nearby sat Abang Dolah.

Adi and his friends hung around the tent. After a while, a rather smartly attired man with a badge bearing the goat with horns logo went up on the stage. Everyone applauded. The four boys also clapped, even though they didn't know who he was. Then, the man started to speak in a husky and firm voice.

"Merdeka! Merdeka! Merdeka!" the man cried. The villagers of Kampung Pak Buyung did likewise. Adi joined in, shouting as loud as he could, not knowing what 'liberty' they were referring to. Kassim Boca shouted until the veins of his neck showed. Then all four of them laughed.

"The colonisers are dogs!" the man shouted. "The colonisers must be driven out! Bloodsuckers. Leeches. They drain the people's blood. The white men are bloodsuckers!" The audience was equally spirited. As the man continued with his fiery speech, a radio car entered. Several policemen spilled out of the car and spread out in various directions, but they did nothing to interfere with the rally.

"We want independence," the man on stage continued. "It's our right. The white men can go back to their own country. For too long have they sucked our blood. Bloody colonisers!"

He spoke for a long time. Adi, Kassim Boca, Dolah Supik and Yunos Potek could not fully understand what he was talking about. He would intermittently cry out "Merdeka!" and the villagers would follow suit. Adi noticed that his father would join in as well. Abang Dolah repeatedly thrust a fist into the air as he joined in the chanting.

Adi invited his friends to Alkaff Garden. They all agreed to join him. As they were leaving, the smartly dressed man was still delivering his speech and the audience was still echoing his slogans. The policemen walked about, monitoring the situation. Even as Adi and his friends reached the sarabat stall at the end of the road, the shouts of "Merdeka!" could still be heard.

"They want to oppose the white men," said Dolah Supik.

"Have we got any weapons with which to fight against the white men?" Adi asked.

"The Malays have magic. We can become invisible. We have flying parangs. Later when the people with flying parangs appear, the white men will be finished off," Dolah Supik replied.

"Malays are invincible," said Yunos Potek.

Adi imagined that should it really happen, many white men would die. He imagined how the flying parangs would cut off their heads. Adi was quite horrified that the Malays might really fight the white men. His mother and Abang Dolah had once told him that in the past, when the Malays had fought against the white men, many of the white men's trucks had been overturned. It had happened because the white men had forced a girl who was raised as a Muslim to embrace Christianity. Many white men died, Abang Dolah had said. When the Malays cried *"Allahu Akbar!"* they received a power so strong that they were able to topple over the white men's trucks. Adi was amazed at the strength of the Malays. Sometimes he felt he must also be invincible, like the Malay heroes Abang Dolah talked about.

By the time they arrived at Alkaff Garden, the sun was

directly over their heads. Adi's body had started to reek of sweat. Walking four miles from Kampung Pak Buyung to Alkaff Garden was rather tiring, even though they had stopped to eat sour starfruits or sweet sugarcane along the way.

In the Garden, a group of movie actors was facing a camera. It was a song sequence. The actress was pretty and she wore a glittery dress with sequins. Adi, Kassim Boca, Dolah Supik and Yunos Potek sat on the grass as they watched the actress mime singing; no sound actually came from her mouth. Every now and then, a fat man who wore a cap would ask her to stop. She would then resume "singing" and the scene went on for a very long time. Adi started to feel bored. He and his friends moved on to the lake; many children were bathing there. They then headed to their usual hangout, next to a banyan tree that had roots sprawling right into the lake. From the top of the banyan tree they were able to jump into the cold water. There was plenty of moss in the lake and lots of fish too.

After about two hours, they climbed onto the bank to dry themselves, and then walked up a nearby hill. Dolah Supik pointed out: "This is where P. Ramlee acted in the film *Sarjan Hassan*."

Adi sat atop the hill and daydreamed of being Sergeant Hassan, who had fought against the Japanese in World War II. He picked up a crooked twig that looked like a pistol, and pretended to shoot at Kassim Boca, Yunos

Potek and Dolah Supik.

Exhausted, they finally left Alkaff Garden. The film crew was gone. Adi and his friends were worn out and walked home wearily. When they arrived at Kampung Pak Buyung, the people from the People's Party were no longer there. The tent was empty. Several of the coconut leaves that had been tied to the tent-poles had fallen to the ground. The chairs were all stacked up. All was calm again. Adi bade his friends goodbye and walked home, feeling hungry and thirsty. He wanted to go home and stuff himself until he felt full.

• • •

That evening, after his meal, Adi climbed the banyan tree near his house. A strong wind was blowing and several monitor lizards scuttled to seek for cover in its roots. He looked around at the surrounding scenery, at the attap- and zinc-roofed houses of the village. The houses on stilts at Lorong 3 appeared hazy. The Cathay Building stood tall and prominent in the distance. Adi had never watched a movie at Cathay, even though he really wanted to go there, because the tickets were expensive. He looked at the building for a long time. The roof of the Chinese barracks near where Kak Salmah lived was clearly visible; it was made of orange ceramic tiles, and several torn kites were trapped in its crevices. A blue bird landed on a branch near Adi. It turned its head to the left and then to the right, then it flew away and landed next to the coconut-husk peeler's attap-roofed house. Adi could see the piles of husks that had been flattened, to be made later into brooms. Adi leant back against the trunk of the banyan tree to rest, and found some numbers inscribed in the bark, as well as some Chinese characters and the picture of a dragon. Below him, three Chinese men were digging a hole in the ground, right next to the banyan tree. He studied them closely, wondering what it was they wanted to bury.

The men dug a hole that was about a foot deep. They placed some newspapers inside the cavity. Then they put in several bulbs containing liquid, parangs, bicycle chains and knives. Abang Dolah had often told him that members of secret societies would bury their weapons in that same spot; they would later use these acid-bulbs and blades to fight other gangs. Therefore, when such weapons were buried in the day, it meant there would be a clash between gangs in the evening.

After the weapons were covered up, the men looked around to make sure that no one was watching, then they left. Many of Adi's neighbours knew about these activities of the secret societies, but no one bothered about it. Adi and his neighbours did not wish to mess with them.

When they had gone, Adi climbed down the tree. He then told his mother what he saw.

"You might fall down the tree and die. That banyan tree is haunted, you know," chided his mother. "And if those men had noticed you, they might have killed you."

Adi remained silent.

His mother continued, "Where's your sister? She has been out since morning and still hasn't come home. I really wonder where her behaviour comes from. Perhaps from your father. What sort of girl is so fond of spending time in other people's houses? Maybe she's eager to get married. Go and find her."

ACCIDENTS DO HAPPEN

ADI HEADED OUT to look for his sister. He first went to Kak Salmah's house, but his sister was not there. Kak Salmah was not at home either, but her daughter Jamilah was doing laundry. There were bruises on her face, which made her look awful. Adi saw the empty bottles of stout in the rubbish bin in front of Kak Salmah's door, stashed under some durian skins.

As usual, he dropped by the kolong of Pak Abas's house. Dolah Supik was there. He was clad in his usual dark blue singlet, grey shorts, and slippers so worn out that the soles of his feet appeared to touch the ground. He was tall, had long toes and his fingernails were dirty. Adi stared at Dolah Supik's nails as the latter scratched his cheek.

"Let's go scrounge for aluminium," Dolah Supik proposed.

"Where?" asked Adi.

"Kallang Puding, the bus factory," Dolah Supik replied, adding, "Tonight's ten-cent movie at Jalan Alsagoff is great. It's called *Pontianak*!"

Dolah Supik and Adi left the kolong. Adi felt very short as he walked next to Dolah Supik, who had to stop to adjust his slippers when the toe-grip snapped off. It was not too far from Kampung Pak Buyung to Kallang Puding, only a thirty-minute walk to their favourite destination. There were many factories in the area that specialised in bus assembly, as well as welding workshops. As a result, a lot of scrap aluminium was discarded outside the buildings, and became a source of income for Adi and Dolah Supik. A kati of aluminium could fetch a price of thirty-five cents. Brass brought in sixty cents per kati. Copper would fetch an even higher price at eighty cents per kati.

Adi walked along, whistling softly. He looked forward to watching the ten-cent movie *Pontianak* later in the evening, munching on turnip and opak again.

"If we can't get anything, we can steal the Sikhs' pots," Dolah Supik suggested.

After picking up several pieces of scrap aluminium, Adi and Dolah Supik headed towards Alkaff Garden. They walked through backyards and the outdoor kitchen areas of the rich folk who lived there, on the lookout for aluminium basins, kettles or brass trays placed or hung on fences in the backyards. Adi was quite used to stealing these items by now. He would even go into vacant houses and pull out the electrical wiring, melt the wires, and then sell the copper inside. Stealing, pilfering and taking without permission—all these had become second nature.

The two circled around Alkaff Garden and walked along the back lanes. Once in a while, they climbed over the fences, into the wealthy residents' yards, to pluck mangoes, starfruits or guavas. This way, they were still able to fill their hungry stomachs even while wandering about. By evening, they had managed to gather an estimated one dollar and sixty cents worth of items between them, enough not only for a movie but also for turnip, opak and fried nuts. Dolah Supik could also afford to buy a pack of Poker cigarettes at twenty-five cents.

They went their separate ways after deciding to meet again at half past six at the Kampung Pak Buyung sarabat stall.

Adi returned home to find his mother in a rage, scolding his sister who had finally come home. Ani's eyes were swollen as if she had been crying.

"If your father finds out, you'll be dead. Useless child! Bringing shame to your parents. Who's the bloody guy? Tell me, who is the bloody guy?"

His sister remained quiet and still.

"Speak up, damned child! You want to die? You bitch! If you want to get married, just say so!"

Ani dried her tears on the sleeve of her faded baju kurung. Adi was puzzled when he saw his sister being scolded in such a manner by his mother. He did not understand why she was being so severely reprimanded.

"You're another one," Adi's mother said, now turning on him. "So poor in your studies, and for the past month of school holidays you've done nothing but wander around. If you get arrested someday, then you know. Curse you both! You're nothing but trouble!" She picked up a broom and made after him. Adi fled to the kitchen to save himself. His mother turned back to Ani. The broom landed on her head repeatedly and she squirmed in pain.

"As for your father, always gambling, day and night. Non-stop. He doesn't even know that his daughter is pregnant." She paused for a moment, then called, "Adi! Adi! Come here!" When he did not show himself, she became angrier. She entered the kitchen to beat him. He darted out and scrambled up the banyan tree and out of his mother's reach. After some time, Adi remembered his appointment with Dolah Supik; he quickly climbed down the tree and ran towards the sarabat stall.

• • •

That evening, when Adi returned after watching the movie *Pontianak*, he saw that Abang Dolah had come to visit his parents. With him were a woman of about thirty-five years old and a man of about fifty. The woman was wearing a shawl. They both looked like Indians, with dark complexions and high noses. Adi quickly slipped into the house. His sister was sitting in a corner of her room, crying. A classical song was playing from Ah Kong's radio next door. Adi's ear pricked up as he tried to overhear the conversation between his parents and their visitors. He was certain that something momentous had happened. He also sensed that his sister had done something wrong.

"We must now settle these youngsters," Abang Dolah said.

"We should just marry them off as soon as possible, that would be better," the dark-skinned woman replied.

"Yes indeed, but what about the wedding costs? What about the dowry? We can't afford to give everything away!" Abang Dolah retorted.

"We're also poor," the dark-skinned woman said. "My brother works for the Harbour Board. We're willing to give three hundred dollars for wedding expenses. Our side is not going to hold any celebration or event. That's all we can afford. What can we do? Accidents happen. We must do something about these youngsters quickly, before people start talking about them."

Adi's mother was in tears. His father remained quiet.

"All right then, when will the solemnisation be held?" Abang Dolah asked.

"Next week, we'll come again," said the Indian man. "We'll fix the date then."

That night, after they all had left, Adi's father blew his top.

"Damned child! Such a bitch! Want to be a whore?" Adi's father screamed, kicking and hitting his sister. "You bring shame to your parents! We're already poor, barely able to feed ourselves. I go out to earn a living all day and night. Is this how you repay me?" Ani tried to find safety in her mother's lap. "Damned child! Get out of here! Get lost! If not, I'll kill you, I don't mind losing a child, get lost!"

Adi's mother tried to prevent him from hitting Ani

anymore, but his father turned around and slapped her.

"You're the same, what kind of a mother are you? You can't even look after a single daughter. You pamper her, give her attention, now when she's brought us shame, where will you want to hide your face?" His father shifted his attention back to Ani and tried to hit her again. She got up and then ran away quickly into the darkness outside, fading away as she passed the street lamp next to the coconut-husk peeler's house. Adi went after her, to bring her back, but he was unable to catch up with her. His mother cried while his father continued to scold both his sister and mother. Adi felt afraid and was worried that his father's wrath would turn on him.

After that incident, Adi's sister did not return home. He understood from the conversations he overheard that his sister had eloped to live with her lover in Tembeling Road. Adi had no idea where that was. His father did not bother to look for her. His mother often cried, thinking about the whole affair. The dark-skinned woman and man did not come back to their house. After three months or so, Adi heard from his mother that his sister had married the Indian Peranakan who worked for the Harbour Board.

Although they had hardly been close, he still felt her absence. Now, it was only him and his parents. His father's gambling habit became worse. Sometimes Pak Mat did not return home until morning. Adi was often sent to look for him. When he saw his father gambling, Adi would ask him to come home. He would also ask for money, for household expenses. Most of the time, his father would simply chase him away. Once, Pak Mat slapped him for disturbing him when he had been gambling; Adi had scampered away, crying. He was extremely sad at the thought of his family's plight. At those times, he would climb up the banyan tree and cry his heart out amid its branches.

• • •

Mak Timah was sewing a dress, slowly and meticulously, by the light of a kerosene lamp. Adi was looking out at the banyan tree. The light from the street lamp next to the coconut-husk peeler's house threw the tree into silhouette, and Adi supposed that this was the time of day when the spirits came out of it. The serpents would sneak out of their cavity; Adi imagined them to be as big as the trunk of a coconut tree. Their eyes would certainly be bulging, and they might even have horns, like dragons. Some people said the banyan tree was hundreds of years old, but the spirits who dwelled within were certainly older than that. Adi wondered whether the spirits would eat the oranges and eggs left as offerings by the Chinese people who worshipped there.

Adi's father was lying down on the ambin. He was wearing only a sarong. Adi turned away from his father as he saw Bibik arriving with kuih bakul, a rice cake normally served during Chinese New Year; she was in her white kebaya and a matching brown floral batik sarong. Bibik greeted Mak Timah and then asked what she was doing.

"Sewing," replied Mak Timah.

"So how, have you made up your mind about Busuk's child?"

Of late, Mak Timah had been considering adopting Busuk's child. Ever since Ani had left the house, she had been feeling lonely. She wondered whether she ought to believe the datuk's prediction, that the child would bring bad luck. *But he is not Allah*, she reasoned. She said nothing as yet to Bibik, instead passing her the betel holder.

Bibik took a betel leaf, dressed it with chalk, stuffed it into her right cheek, and began to slowly munch on it, making her cheek look swollen.

"Busuk is due to give birth in a month's time," Bibik said. "Please take the child. We'll pay for all the delivery costs, as well as the cost of the birth certificate and the fees for oath-taking. We will also give you two hundred and fifty dollars, on top of that."

Pak Mat jumped to his feet when he heard Bibik mention the money. "In that case, can. When will she deliver?"

"In a month's time," Bibik replied.

"Have you given this serious thought?" Mak Timah asked Pak Mat.

He ignored her and went on, addressing Bibik, "Can, but could you also help to pay for milk until the child stops drinking milk?"

"Sure! Sure!" Bibik nodded.

"In that case, I agree to adopt Busuk's child," Pak Mat

told her. Bibik was elated. She cursed her daughter out loud. Busuk had believed in the medium's predictions that her child would bring bad luck!

• • •

Two months later, Busuk's baby became Mak Timah's adopted daughter. The child looked physically normal, though she was extremely small; she had weighed only two and a half pounds at birth. Busuk did not visit her child at all once she was handed over to Mak Timah. Pak Mat used the two hundred and fifty dollars Bibik gave them to gamble, and Mak Timah did not receive a single cent. Mak Timah called Busuk's daughter "Pungut". Her legal Malay name was Zaharah, and her Chinese name was Yap Swee Hong; the letter of oath had been secured, but Mak Timah also kept the birth certificate, which had Pungut's Chinese name on it. Adi did not feel anything had changed since the arrival of Pungut into his family; Mak Timah was kept busy looking after her, while Pak Mat did not care at all about her presence. As far as Adi was concerned, Pungut made no difference to his life.

Adi's sister Ani never visited Mak Timah, although Abang Dolah as usual often came by. As for Adi, his life went on as usual. He spent his time climbing the banyan tree and stealing aluminium and copper.

THE DIVORCEE WITH THREE CHILDREN

IT HAD BEEN two days since Pak Mat last came home. Mak Timah was furious and constantly complained about him.

"Does he want to die? Gambling day and night," she grumbled, then added, "Adi, go find your father."

Adi was confused. He had no idea where his father had gone. Perhaps he could find him at his workplace, under the Merdeka Bridge near Kallang Airport.

Adi put on his worn-out slippers. Clad in his faded singlet and blue school shorts, he left. He walked along Lorong 23; Chinese families lived on both sides of the street, and it was only at the end of the street that one could find a Malay family. His friend Yahya lived here. Yahya's father was a trishaw pedaller and his plump sister worked as a waitress at a bar in Lorong 29. Adi saw Yahya's sister as he walked along; she was dressed in a sarong that exposed her shoulders and the upper part of her chest. Her face was covered with powder.

Adi entered Lorong 18 and passed the junction with Mountbatten Road. He trudged along until he at last reached the Merdeka Bridge where it spanned the Kallang

River. There, he approached the security guard and asked for his father. The guard instructed him to walk straight ahead until he reached the place where the ships were berthed. When Adi reached the shipyard, he found Pak Mat busy painting a ship a flat grey colour.

"Ma wants you to come home," Adi said.

"You go home first," Pak Mat replied. "I'll come once I've finished work."

Adi returned all the way home to relay his father's message, which made Mak Timah grumble. That night, Pak Mat did not come home. Mak Timah became angrier. This time, she decided to find him herself. She put on a shawl and a faded baju kurung, as well as a faded batik sarong. Mak Timah stepped out into the night, leaving Adi to take care of the house and Pungut.

The well was in darkness. The hibiscus tree that shaded the area in the daytime was also cloaked in black. Only the silhouettes of the well and hibiscus flowers were hazily visible in the moonlight. The stars twinkled overhead, and Tong San's children were busy playing nearby among themselves. They were jumping about and shouting dialogue from some Chinese opera.

Mak Timah first stopped at Abang Dolah's house. In his white singlet, he played his violin, and the song, "Sri Banang", touched her. The small kerosene lamp inside Abang Dolah's room gave out only a dim light. Abang Dolah saw Mak Timah watching him, and stopped his music.

"Do you know where Pak Mat is?" she asked, straightening her shawl.

Abang Dolah put down the violin and thought for a while. "If he's not at the sarabat stall, try Bibi's house at Lorong 21." The mention of Bibi's name made Mak Timah's blood boil. He added, "Why didn't you ask Adi to accompany you at this hour of the night?"

"Who will look after Pungut? Moreover, what's there for me to be afraid of? I'm not wearing any gold jewellery. I'm not a young girl. Who would want to rape me? I'm leaving now."

Abang Dolah stared after her, bewildered.

Mak Timah knew that Bibi, the divorcée who had three children, was indeed fond of entertaining other women's husbands. The dark-skinned woman was an avid gambler and loved to gather married men in her house. The image of Bibi's dark face, fluffy hair and fleshy hips flashed before Mak Timah's eyes. She walked quickly by the dim light of the street lamps. As she passed Bongkok's shop, two dogs looked up at her. She took no notice of them and continued walking.

At the Kampung Pak Buyung sarabat stall, several men were gambling. Mak Timah saw Yusoff Gemuk, Mail Sengau, Daud Cina, Mama Sulaiman and Ali Spring there. She did not see Pak Mat. She moved on, walking along Aljunied Road. A few cars and buses passed by. The traffic lights shone brightly on Mak Timah's sour face. She walked hurriedly past Geylang Craft Centre and turned onto Lorong 21. The smell of toast from a bakery nearby filled the air. Bright light came from the pressure lamps and kerosene lamps of the Malay homes there. The night was still young.

Bibi's house was located directly behind the bakery. It was a small house. The door was ajar, and the light from a flickering carbide lamp lit up the entrance. Mak Timah walked up to the door and knocked on it. She then immediately pushed it open and saw Pak Mat and Bibi inside, both with playing cards in their hands. Glasses of coffee and fried peanuts were laid out on two tables. None of Bibi's children were at home. Pak Mat was clearly surprised to see Mak Timah.

"You are playing cards, are you?" Mak Timah yelled. "And after cards, what will you play? You don't even bother to come home, what kind of a husband are you! You have no sense of responsibility at all! Bloody old man!"

She then turned to Bibi. "So, you indeed keep other women's husbands! Bitch! Loose divorcée!" Pak Mat quickly stood up and moved towards Mak Timah to prevent her from entering further, and then dragged her outside.

"Who is keeping your husband?" Bibi retaliated, still seated. "You think he's so rich that I want to keep him? Be careful of what you say. You can't even look after your own husband."

"Loose divorcée! *Frisky* divorcée!" Mak Timah yelled again. She then turned to run after Pak Mat, who had already started walking away. Pak Mat walked faster to avoid her and increase the distance between them. Mak Timah kept grumbling and cursing as she chased after him. Several passers-by were puzzled, thinking she was talking to herself. Pak Mat continued to walk faster. Mak Timah ran as fast as she could. Pak Mat did not look back even once. Mak Timah's shawl kept slipping and she had to keep straightening it. The chase lasted until they both reached home.

"So old but still a womaniser," Mak Timah lashed at him the moment she entered the house. "You've fallen for that woman. Gambling and never coming home. What have you been fed by her?"

Pak Mat remained silent. He took a deep puff of his Poker cigarette. Ah Kong's Rediffusion was still on next door. The voice of Tong San's daughter was audible. She continued to play, singing phrases from Chinese operas.

Adi could only watch the drama that was unfolding between his parents. Pungut was sleeping soundly. Suddenly, Mak Timah lunged at Pak Mat. She hit him on the chest repeatedly. Pak Mat pushed her away. She fell, sitting hard on the uneven ground. Mak Timah got up and flew at him again. Again, Pak Mat pushed her away. This time Mak Timah fell on the ambin. Adi watched the fight between his parents, and tried to keep the tears from escaping his eyes.

"No sense of responsibility, lusting after that bitch. If you've really fallen for her, go! Take your clothes and belongings and go live with that woman."

Pak Mat remained motionless. Mak Timah continued to rant. Only when the sounds of Ah Kong's Rediffusion and the voices of Tong San's children faded, did she quieten down. She then went into the room where Pungut was sleeping and began crying uncontrollably. Pak Mat was still sitting on the ambin. He continued to smoke one cigarette after another.

Adi's heart always fell when he saw his parents fighting. There was no longer any peace in the house, but he was unable to do anything other than watch her crying. In his heart, he cursed his father for his cruel behaviour. Not coming home for days. Gambling all day and all night. The money he gave them was never enough. Adi and his mother often went hungry. It was fortunate that Bibik gave thirty dollars every month for Pungut's milk, otherwise she too would have gone hungry. Adi's father gave Mak Timah only fifty dollars for expenses, including for kerosene to cook and to fill in the kerosene lamps, although the lamp in the kitchen needed replacing; the glass was broken and only half its chimney was intact. Fifty dollars a month was simply not enough to buy rice, sugar, coffee, fish, vegetables, tamarind and salt.

Adi, who was almost always famished, would often eat outside with the money he earned by selling stolen aluminium. Sometimes when he was hungry, Dolah Supik or Yunos Potek would treat him to a piece of prata. With that, he would be able to bear his hunger for a while. At other times, he and Mak Timah would often have plain tea into which they would dip sweet biscuits. Sometimes his mother would make plain pancakes, which contained nothing but flour. Pak Mat did not care about their hunger.

Sometimes Adi would steal his father's money. There would be lots of coins in his father's trousers pocket whenever Pak Mat won at gambling. At times there would be rolls of one-dollar notes in the pockets, but Adi would take only the coins. That way, his father would not notice that his money had been stolen. Adi had not gotten new clothes in a long time, not even for Hari Raya, the holiday marking the end of the month of fasting. Mak Timah also hardly got new clothes; Kak Salmah, whom people referred to as a loose woman, often gave Mak Timah her hand-me-downs. When Adi's sister had been around, she had also suffered the same fate; she too had often been famished and she seldom got new clothes. Perhaps that had been the reason why she liked to spend her time at other people's houses. That way, she could get something to sate her hunger. She used to spend a lot of time at Eton's house, Bibah's house, Kak Salmah's house, and Hendon's house, and sometimes they gave his sister their old dresses.

Adi sometimes puzzled at the way their family suffered. His father was, in fact, gainfully employed as a ship painter with the Public Works Department and he earned a hundred and twenty dollars a month. If only his father did not gamble, Adi was certain that his life would be comfortable.

He had a friend named Sairi, whose father who worked as a gardener. Yet Sairi was never famished. Another friend, Basri also never complained of hunger even though his father was just a lowly driver. But Sairi's father was pious and prayed regularly, and Basri's father was gentle and affectionate towards his family. How fortunate Sairi and Basri were, thought Adi.

• • •

That night Adi found it hard to sleep. Mak Timah had already fallen asleep next to Pungut. His father was snoring on the ambin, shirtless. Adi was restless. He could faintly hear the song "Sri Banang" coming from Abang Dolah's violin. Adi climbed down from the ambin, walked through the house and peered into the kitchen. It was dark, as the lamp had gone out. It had perhaps run out of kerosene. Moonlight lit up the bathroom. Adi noticed the water jar was half-empty. He resolved to refill it the next day.

Adi then went out. Tong San's house was already dark and the only light around came from the kerosene lamp inside Abang Dolah's house. Adi walked towards the light. When Abang Dolah opened the door, Adi entered, sullen faced.

"What's wrong, Adi?"

"I can't sleep, Abang Dolah."

"Are you worried about something?"

"No."

"Sad?"

"No."

"Hungry?"

"No."

"Don't think too much. Life won't be joyful if you think too much. Look at me, my life is more difficult than yours." Adi kept quiet, and stared at Abang Dolah's violin as it lay on the ambin. Abang Dolah lit up one of his Poker cigarettes and then blew out rings of smoke.

"I have a hard life. I'm divorced, my child is not with me, I'm living on welfare! I'm worse off. It's depressing!"

"You're smart, but purposely refuse to work," Adi said. "You have a wife, yet you divorced her, and you have a lover: Kak Habsah!" Abang Dolah broke into laughter. Adi continued, "You're good at casting spells on others, you're good at playing musical instruments." Abang Dolah laughed again.

"That's enough, Adi. Don't think too much. Don't worry so much. Soon, you'll grow up. You study hard. When you're a big man, you will earn well, you will be rich!"

Adi stared at Abang Dolah's face. Without his glasses, his eyes appeared deep-set. His skin was fair, in fact, quite pale. Most of his teeth were blackened with nicotine. His fingers seemed slender and gentle, especially when he played his violin.

Abang Dolah said, "In the past, there was a girl who fell for me when she heard me play the violin." The bright red violin looked beautiful and shone under the light of the lamp. "Let me play a song to entertain you." Abang Dolah took up his violin and played the song "Damak" with great emotion. The beautiful melody made Adi even more melancholy.

· · ·

Adi returned to his room once the night got really quiet. He tried to sleep, but he had lots of things on his mind. His parents' quarrels about his sister, who never came to visit them. Abang Dolah's face with his sunken eyes. The sturdy banyan tree and the increasing number of bird poachers who came to tap its latex. The spirits of the banyan tree. The expression on Kak Salmah's face as she beat Jamilah up. Bongkok's gloomy shop. Starlings, which made a lot of noise as they flew about. Secret societies burying weapons under the banyan tree. Dolah Supik's face as he rode his bicycle. Bibik, who loved to chew betel leaves. The moss-covered well. All these thoughts flashed through his mind one after another.

Adi also remembered he would soon be returning to school. He would walk every day from home to Kota-Kota School. He would soon be meeting his teachers. Faces flashed before his mind's eye. The fierce Cikgu Majid who slapped Adi if he made a mistake in mathematics. Matsom from Lorong 3, who often challenged him to a fight. Rahmat, who always sought his protection when bullied by his friends. He imagined he could hear the school radio programme, in Nona Asiah's voice. All these kept playing in his mind. The gloomy room illuminated by the kerosene lamp. The cracked walls. The smell of Tiger Balm and the stink of Ah Kong's room, next door. Adi looked at the large, intersecting beams under the roof. Several fat lizards were moving here and there. That night, Adi went to sleep after taking a long look at his mother's face. In his sleep, he grit his teeth and cursed his father. He dreamt he was facing the serpent spirits of the banyan tree. Their eyes bored right into his. Adi screamed in his dreams.

THE SKY DARKENS

A LARGE CROWD was gathered in front of the coconut-husk peeler's house. An old bicycle lay flat on the ground. Blocks of ice covered in sawdust had fallen to the ground. Not too far away sprawled a Chinese man, writhing in pain and moaning. He was shirtless and blood trickled down from his head and neck. A saw, used to cut ice, stained with blood, rested next to him.

"He's a member of Gang Eighteen," someone said.

"Some members of Gang Twenty-four must have beaten him up," someone else in the crowd said. Adi now understood what had happened. The ice-peddler had been suspected of being a member of Gang Eighteen, and Gang Twenty-four controlled the area that he had entered. Some members of Gang Twenty-four had apparently bashed him up. After continuing to moan for about fifteen minutes, the young man became motionless.

"Oh no, he's dead!" an onlooker said in Hokkien.

The man did not move for more than five minutes. A police car arrived. Immediately the crowd began to disperse and everyone moved far away from the young ice-peddler. The policemen covered the unmoving man with some newspaper, given to them by Bibik. A short while later, an ambulance arrived, although it did not stay.

Half an hour later, a hearse came to carry away the dead body. The police officers were still busy questioning the coconut-husk peeler as to whether he had seen anyone kill the young man. The coconut-husk peeler only shook his head. All the people who were interrogated by the police said they knew and saw nothing. The kuih bakul that had been kept on the ground to dry by the coconut-husk peeler had gotten trampled by the crowd and were damaged.

Adi sat on the ambin outside his house. He saw the hearse take away the corpse of the young Chinese man. Usually, when such deaths occurred, there would be a massive gang clash afterwards. The gang to which the dead man had belonged would certainly want revenge against the members of the rival gang who had killed him.

Adi remembered the weapons buried under the banyan tree: the acid-filled bulbs, the parangs, knives and bicycle chains. These objects would sooner or later be dug up and used by the relevant secret society.

• • •

Night fell. The banyan tree was dark and illuminated only by the street lamp next to the coconut-husk peeler's house. Everyone stayed indoors that night, fearing a clash between the gangs. Every now and then, Adi would peek out from the slits in the wall to see if anything was happening. Abang Dolah was at Adi's house as well, animatedly telling Adi and Mak Timah about the secret societies. Pak Mat was not at home. Adi had no inkling of whether or not his father would return. Despite the quarrel between his parents the other night, Pak Mat's attitude had remained unchanged. Mak Timah became taciturn and could not be bothered to lecture Pak Mat anymore. If he wished to return, so be it. If he did not, it would make no difference.

Abang Dolah now started talking about pontianak, cackling female ghosts that fed on the blood of living men. Adi listened attentively.

"A long time ago, someone married a pontianak who had turned back into a living woman," said Abang Dolah. "The woman was pretty. She had a child after her marriage, and one day, while her child was searching for lice on the mother's head, the child saw a nail. When she pulled the nail out, the mother screamed and turned into a pontianak again.

"Every Thursday night, the pontianak would return to look for her husband, who lived in fear of her. She would leave scratches on the door of her husband's house. Then, a medium was called in to chase her away, and after that the pontianak only dared to appear at a distance. Her cackle can still be heard from far away on Thursday nights, especially during a full moon when cananga or frangipani flowers are blooming." Story complete, Abang Dolah took a sip of the thick coffee that Mak Timah had brewed for him.

Adi heard the voices of the crowd outside his house. He peeped out and saw several men digging up the ground where they had buried their weapons. Each of them had tied a strip of white cloth around their heads. Adi estimated that there were about fifteen of them. Each held a weapon in their hands. Some carried parangs. Some held metal pipes. Some were armed with bicycle chains. Some had bulbs that were filled with acid. Abang Dolah and Mak Timah also took turns to peer outside. The gang gathered under the banyan tree and had a discussion.

Around midnight, Abang Dolah woke Adi up. There was a commotion outside. When Adi looked through the slit on the wall, he saw two groups of people fighting each other. Just like in the movies, there were slashings, beatings, shouts and screams. Many people appeared to have collapsed. As soon as they heard the siren of the police car, those who were still fighting scattered. The injured and wounded gang members were carried away in an ambulance and the situation started to calm down. Yet no one in the village dared to come out. They had all witnessed the drama from the slits in the walls of their respective houses.

• • •

In the morning, Adi saw many bloodstains on the ground in front of his house. He felt quite horrified when he recalled the images of the wounded. Some would probably die later, he thought. Nevertheless, the incident soon faded from his mind. This was not the first time he had seen secret societies fighting and such incidents had become commonplace to the residents here. A few months ago, as Adi was buying coffee at Ah Kong's shop, the oldest coffee shop around, a fight broke out. All of the gang members were young. They demanded "protection money" from Ah Kow. His sons confronted them. As a result, one of Ah Kow's sons was stabbed with an ice pick and had to be rushed to the hospital. Fortunately, he survived.

Another time, Adi saw a clash between some gangs in front of a bar at Lorong 25. Two men's stomachs were slashed open. One man's head was smashed in with a metal pipe, and he died.

The only positive thing about it all was that the secret societies never disturbed the residents of the village. They knew them very well. Still, Adi had to be careful whenever he walked by Lorong 25 or Lorong 27. He could not leave his shirt unbuttoned, or wear a chain around his neck, let alone have tattoos on his body. If he did, the secret society members who controlled that area would certainly beat him up.

That Friday, many people gathered under the banyan tree. Adi changed his mind about climbing the tree, and approached the crowd instead. Apparently, his Chinese neighbour, who was nicknamed Opium-Smoker Uncle, had hung himself from the banyan tree.

The hanging roots of the tree were twisted around his neck. Opium-Smoker Uncle's lean figure appeared very light as it swayed; his tongue jutted out and his eyes bulged. Blood oozed from his mouth, dripping down his chin. In the midst of it all, a fat Chinese man took advantage of the gathering to pick betting numbers right under Opium-Smoker Uncle's hanging corpse. As a crowd gathered, he quickly left, with his numbers. After that incident, many people did not dare to go about at night. Mak Timah would scold Adi whenever she saw him climb the banyan tree.

Soon after that, another terrifying incident occurred. Tong Samboo's daughter, a plump eighteen-year-old girl, tried to kill herself by drinking Clorox bleach. She was taken to the hospital, foaming at the mouth. Mak Timah said that her own brother had raped the poor girl. The police came to investigate. Adi eventually saw Tong Samboo's son, hands cuffed behind his back, being pushed into a police car one evening. When Tong Samboo's daughter was discharged from the hospital, she looked like a deranged person. Stricken by trauma, she would lift up her dress and show her private parts to people who passed by her house. Even Adi had seen her do that. Tong Samboo cried, thinking about her children's plight. Her husband had died a long time ago, and all she had were her two children. Her daughter too would cry for what had happened.

• • •

Chinese New Year was just a week away. There was a festive

atmosphere around Adi's house. Everywhere firecrackers would sizzle, like rice being fried. Many people burnt firecrackers under the banyan tree, and the ground was littered with their remnants. Adi would wait to see which ones did not explode; he would pick them up later and set them off. The smell of sulphur filled the air. Sometimes, he would remove the sulphur gunpowder from inside several firecrackers and pour it into a bottle. He would then attach a wick to the bottle and throw it. It would explode like a hand grenade. Adi would be very excited, as if he had thrown a real bomb.

There were lots of children carrying lanterns. Kuih bakul dried in the sun outside many houses. Adi was quite happy to see the Chinese children playing with the firecrackers and carrying lanterns. When Chinese New Year came each year, Bibik would send over Mandarin oranges, Chinese cakes, as well as ang pow to Adi's house. Adi was happy to receive the red packets with money inside.

In the midst of all the celebrations, Abang Dolah often dropped by to talk about the coming General Elections. Abang Dolah asked Mak Timah and anyone else who would listen to vote for the goat's head logo party. At times, Adi noticed Abang Dolah would visit the residents' homes, going house to house together with several people who wore the flame logo badge. Sometimes members of the axe logo party would be present too. The elections were around the corner. Adi heard from Abang Dolah that they wanted to drive the white men out from the country. They wanted to be independent. The white men were colonisers, Abang Dolah said.

Adi did not quite understand what Abang Dolah meant, or why they needed to drive the white men out. Still, Adi enjoyed watching all those people speak in their tents, on a stage lit by a generator-powered lamp. Adi would join in shouting "Merdeka!" loudly whenever the speaker on the stage shouted the word. The people of Kampung Pak Buyung also liked to come together if there was a rally. The villagers welcomed all speakers; the members of the goat's head, flame, and axe logo parties, all were welcome. Everyone would shout "Merdeka!" When these election campaigners arrived to give their speeches, there would be a festive atmosphere at Kampung Pak Buyung. The Chinese rojak seller would set up his stall near the tent, as would the Indian bean seller, the Chinese roast squid seller and the Chinese ice-cream seller. Many people would gather. They would shout, *"Merdeka! Merdeka! Merdeka!"*

Adi saw a lot of posters being pasted onto coconut trees and the rusty zinc fence of the well. These were posters supporting the candidates for the various parties, including the goat's head logo party. There also were posters with the warship logo, the axe logo, and horned buffalo logo. These days, Abang Dolah seldom came over to Adi's house. But, whenever he did come, he would talk about the General Elections. Abang Dolah explained that the white men had been ruling the country for too long. In the past, he said,

when the Japanese had invaded, the white men had not
fought all out, but simply surrendered; he said that one
Japanese man was able to control one hundred white men,
even force them to eat snails. The Japanese had stripped
the white men of their shirts and then forced them to walk
barefoot for hundreds of miles, from Jurong to Changi.
The Japanese, Abang Dolah pointed out, had known
how to teach a lesson to the white men, who had been
interested only in amassing riches to be brought back to
their homeland.

Mak Timah found Abang Dolah's ideas ridiculous. She
said their people could not govern a country, not produce
even a single needle. As a result, she and Abang Dolah
would argue heatedly until late into the night.

Pak Mat remained unchanged. He still gambled.
Sometimes he would come home and sometimes he
would not. People no longer gossiped about Adi's sister
eloping with the Harbour Board employee. It became
clear that something was wrong with Pungut; she did not
grow. She kept shaking her head in a peculiar way and
making a droning noise, like a mosquito. People who saw
her compared her to a loktang, a Taoist monk who goes
into a trance to carry out exorcisms. Mak Timah was sad,
but she held on to the hope that Pungut would grow up to
be like other children. She would scold anyone who said
that Pungut was not normal.

• • •

Adi started going back to school. He would walk there daily. The Kota-Kota Malay School was located next to a river. The students of the school grew restless as the General Elections drew near. It was generally said that the axe logo party members wanted to set up a Malay Secondary School here. Generally, the Malay students studied only till Primary Seven and they learned skills such as sewing, basket-weaving and gardening. Upon graduation, they would become labourers or policemen. Adi was taken in by what his friends said; he told Mak Timah that he did not want to be a policeman upon completing his studies. Abang Dolah too said that it was important for Malay students to continue to study further, to become doctors, lawyers and engineers.

"What kind of doctor do you want to be?" Mak Timah said, sarcastically. "A doctor who dissects pigs? Just become a labourer. A policeman is even better."

Adi was upset because Mak Timah failed to understand the ideas of the axe logo party members. He felt insulted by his mother's words. Adi aspired to be a doctor or lawyer.

That evening, when Adi walked past Tong Samboo's house, her daughter was railing at passers-by even as she exposed her private parts to them. He went back and forth a few times.

The sky darkened. Heavy clouds moved in quickly, despite being laden with rain. A mad wind was blowing. The leaves of the banyan tree rustled in the wind. Adi looked at the sky and saw several groups of birds flying about in search of shelter. The dark clouds were becoming thicker. And then, it started to rain.

"Take a pail to collect the rainwater in the room," Mak Timah ordered. "The roof is leaking!"

The rainwater seeped through the rusty zinc roof in many places, then dripped onto the rubber mat on the ambin. Adi got a basin.

"There are many leaks. How to catch all the water?" Adi asked.

"The towkay of this house knows how to collect rent, yet he's dodgy in repairing the leaks," mumbled Mak Timah.

The old, cracked walls of the house were damp with rain. Adi ran his fingers over a wall and noticed a small hole in it. Adi peeped through the hole and into Ah Kong's house and saw him sleeping under a mosquito net. He also peeped into Tong Samboo's house and saw her sitting on a stool, her knees pulled close to her chest. She was eating porridge. Several basins and pails were laid out in a row, on the floor, to catch the rainwater. Adi then shifted to the windows. The windows were open and the rain splattered onto his face. He closed the windows and peeped out through the hole in the wall, at the banyan tree. The rain was getting heavier. Water dripped down the roots of the banyan tree. That day, it rained incessantly until evening. By the time the rain began to abate, the street lamp next to the coconut-husk peeler's house had come on. The night was cold after the rain. Adi was hungry. Mak Timah made plain tea for him, and Adi dipped his plain biscuits into it.

"Don't finish it all now, or you will be famished tomorrow," Mak Timah cautioned him. "And leave some for me." Adi's stomach was still craving for more. The cold of the night cut deeper into his bones.

GOING TO NEW WORLD
OR TO GREAT WORLD

EVER SINCE SCHOOL reopened, Adi could scrounge for aluminium only on Saturdays and Sundays. Also, he no longer had Dolah Supik to keep him company, since his friend had gotten a job as a drum-pusher, working irregular hours as a daily-wage worker. It was, however, good that Dolah Supik was now employed because every weekend he would treat Adi to prata at the sarabat stall, and then invite Adi to watch a ten-cent movie at Jalan Alsagoff. If the movie was not good, they would go to another show at Lorong 31. Sometimes Dolah Supik would invite Adi to join him for sightseeing at the New World or Great World amusement parks. Adi really enjoyed the bright lights, playing bumper cars and going into the ghost house. Sometimes, the two friends would spend several hours at one place or the other.

Dolah Supik was one of Adi's best friends. Although he was already working, he never forgot Adi. Adi really felt indebted to Dolah Supik. Adi found his broad face, the way he talked fast and his generosity endearing. Dolah Supik also taught Adi how to ride his full-sized men's bicycle. Sometimes Adi would rent a bicycle at ten cents an hour. This bicycle was usually easier to ride as it was smaller than Dolah Supik's bicycle and his feet could touch the ground. Dolah Supik would sometimes give Adi some money for his school fees, which was twenty-five cents per month. Adi felt a deep affection for Dolah Supik. He felt that Dolah Supik was the kindest person on earth.

That evening Adi was carrying water from the well. One of his kerosene tins was leaking. It was a clear day and the sun was still bright in the sky. The hibiscus plant beside the wall of the well was flowering. Two or three flowers had already withered. Several buds were about to bloom. A worm emerging from its cocoon caught Adi's attention. The worm was dangling by a fine thread. When Adi looked at the well, he noticed the greenish moss on its walls. The door to Abang Dolah's house was shut, and a pair of ladies' slippers was placed outside the door; Adi was certain that Kak Habsah was inside. Bibik was feeding her ducks, which moved clumsily towards the grains that Bibik scattered. Once in a while, Adi heard peals of laughter from Abang Dolah's room.

Adi poured the water from the kerosene tin into the earthen jar. His mother was bathing Pungut. His father had gone to work. Lately, Pak Mat came home right after work and stayed there. It seemed that Pak Mat had started to change. It was now obvious that he had grown thinner. Mak Timah said Pak Mat had diabetes. Every morning before going to work, Pak Mat would go to the clinic to get an injection, yet he would still drink sweet, thick coffee, which he would ask Adi to buy from Ah Kow's shop.

Adi was sweating profusely. The veins on his arms stood out. His palms were calloused. He went back to the well. Another four tins would fill up the earthen jar, he calculated. As he was crossing in front of Abang Dolah's house, he could again hear Kak Habsah's coquettish laughter. He stopped to rest, sitting on the parapet of the well. He looked up at the clear blue sky. Only a few thin clouds were present. These clouds were moving fast. Usually during the kite-flying season, if the sky were as clear as it was today, several kites would be seen in the sky.

The previous day at school, Adi had overheard the senior students say that the Primary Seven pupils were planning to hold a demonstration so that the government would establish a Malay secondary school. Adi was happy to hear this news. He was looking forward to joining the demonstration. He imagined that if he were sent to an English school, he could become a doctor, a lawyer or an engineer. He then smiled to himself as he remembered that he always got low marks in mathematics. Cikgu Majid would often cane his calf for not memorising his multiplication tables. How could he become a doctor without being able to multiply numbers?

Bibik called out to Adi. He put down his pail and kerosene tins and went to her. She gave him three guavas. Adi smiled at her. He sat next to the well and ate one of the guavas, after which he went back to fetching water. Suddenly, a stocky man in a singlet and grey pants appeared before him.

"Where is Abang Dolah's house?" he asked, fiercely. Adi showed him the way. The stocky man quickly charged at Abang Dolah's door and kicked it in. Adi saw Kak Habsah hastily tying her sarong. Abang Dolah also hurriedly did the same. Kak Habsah's hair was dishevelled. Both Kak Habsah and Abang Dolah were sweating. Kak Habsah's face was pale. Abang Dolah looked as if he had seen a ghost.

"Bitch! Cursed woman! Slut! You've been sleeping around, huh?" The stocky man entered the house to charge at Kak Habsah. He slapped her repeatedly. When Abang Dolah tried to intervene, the stocky man punched him hard in the face. Blood oozed out from Abang Dolah's mouth and nose.

"Bitch! You've been sleeping around!"

"Omar! You useless man!" Kak Habsah yelled. "Divorce me! Divorce me! Useless! Useless!"

Abang Dolah looked around for something he could use as a weapon. He managed to grab hold of the rod used to bar the door.

"You're a political activist? What kind of an activist are you? A shitty one, certainly! Bastard! Keeping another man's wife as mistress!"

Abang Dolah was on guard with his rod. If his opponent charged at him again, he would swing the rod at him. Kak Habsah ran to hide behind Abang Dolah. The stocky man named Omar stood where he was. He looked furious. Sweat trickled down his forehead and neck. Adi could only watch the proceedings from a distance.

"You're a political activist yet you behave like a beast! You have the cheek to lead the people? Would be better for you to lead animals!"

Abang Dolah was still holding tight onto the rod. He adjusted his spectacles. His thin body appeared small compared to Omar. Kak Habsah was still hiding behind him. Using his shirtsleeve, Abang Dolah wiped off the blood that was trickling down from his nose. Red spots of blood, like little thin clouds, stained the sleeve of his T-shirt.

"You charmed my wife, you practised black magic on her. If not, she would not have fallen for you! Bastard! Animal! Come on if you dare!"

"I'm not the one keeping your wife," Abang Dolah calmly replied. "She's the one who came to me. She came to my room. I'm not the one who sought her."

"Cursed woman! Slut! Come back, come back!" the stocky man yelled.

By this time, Tong San had shuffled out of his house to watch the drama unfold. His children were right behind him. Bibik and Busuk had also arrived.

"Enough! Enough! Don't quarrel," Bibik tried to calm them down.

"Coward! Coward!" Kak Habsah screamed. "If you're a man, divorce me! Divorce me! I don't want to come back! You can go to hell! Coward!" She appeared to have become bolder when she saw many people had gathered to watch the commotion. Adi had by now plucked up his courage to get closer to Abang Dolah's house.

"I'll go back, but I'll come back tonight. I will divorce you, you damned woman! But only after I have torn open your stomach and after I have stabbed that coward!"

Omar stormed out of Abang Dolah's room. He passed by Adi as he left. The stench of his sweat made Adi uncomfortable. The man disappeared out of sight behind the well. Tong San and his children left. Bibik also left with Busuk.

"Adi, please go tell Mail Sengau, Daud Cina and Abang Yusoff to come here this evening. Tell them that it's an urgent matter." Adi noticed that both Abang Dolah and Kak Habsah looked exhausted.

When Adi told his mother about the incident, she hurriedly went to Abang Dolah's house and persuaded Kak Habsah to return home with her. Kak Habsah's eyes appeared swollen. Mak Timah boiled some water to dab on her face.

Adi figured that at night, the stocky man would certainly come with his gang from Lorong 21 to attack Abang Dolah. There would be a clash between the people from Lorong 21 and those from Kampung Pak Buyung. Until now, he had never seen Malays fighting Malays, but tonight, he believed he would. He rushed towards the sarabat stall to warn Abang Dolah's friends. In front of Bongkok's shop, two dogs growled and rose up as if to rush at him. Adi stooped to pick up a large stone, and threw it at them. The dogs retreated but continued to growl at him from a distance. Adi continued running. When he reached the sarabat stall, he was panting and his singlet was soaked with sweat, but he was lucky: he found Mail Sengau, Daud Cina, Abang Yusoff and several young men of the village gathered under an angsana tree, chatting and playing checkers or poker. The dried leaves of the angsana had fallen onto the table on which they were gambling. Some people were eating prata.

"Abang Dolah calls you all, he was beaten up by a Lorong 21 man," Adi gasped. "He asks you all to come to his house this evening."

"Who beat him up?" asked Mail Sengau in his nasal voice.

"Kak Habsah's husband, a member of Lorong 21 gang," replied Adi, still breathless.

"Is it bad?" asked Daud Cina.

"Not so bad, but his mouth and nose were bleeding."

"How many people beat him up?" asked Mail Sengau again as he combed his hair.

"One, only one. But tonight he will come again!"

"You go back now. We will come later in the evening," Daud Cina said. As Adi was about to leave, he saw his friend Dolah Supik walking towards him with his bicycle.

"Abang Dolah was beaten up," Adi said.

Dolah Supik asked, wide-eyed, "Was it bad? Who assaulted him? A Chinese?"

"A Lorong 21 gang member, Kak Habsah's husband."

Adi stepped to the back of Dolah Supik's bicycle so as to ride pillion. "Tonight he will come back to attack Abang Dolah again. Abang Dolah has asked Mail Sengau, Daud Cina, and Abang Yusoff to gather at his house tonight. There will surely be a big fight tonight. Do you want to see it?"

Dolah Supik quickly replied, "Of course, of course. Who doesn't want to watch a free show?" Adi climbed onto Dolah Supik's bicycle, and Dolah Supik started to cycle towards Adi's house.

Adi invited Dolah Supik to climb the banyan tree after they left the bicycle against a wall, near a window.

"Let's go up and look at the Cathay Building," Adi said.

"Can see people bathing or not?" asked Dolah Supik as he opened his eyes wide. "Inside the well, inside the latrine?" Adi laughed. Before climbing the tree, Adi grabbed a comb of golden bananas by one of the Chinese villagers as offerings for their deities, and carried them up the tree with him. He could tell that the bananas had just been placed there, as there was no sand on them. The peels were still wet, indicating that they had just been washed.

Dolah Supik gasped for breath as he followed Adi up the banyan tree. The sixteen-year-old youth was like a fish taken out of water and thrown onto land. Adi grinned when he saw Dolah Supik panting.

"Look at Cathay, look at the sky, the clouds are wrestling," said Adi.

"Where's the toilet in which you pass motion? Where's

the well?" asked Dolah Supik.

Adi pointed at the latrines located at the rear of the banana farm. There were three drums in a row. He pointed at the well too.

"Can you see it? If you're lucky there'll be a woman bathing. If it's the coconut-husk peeler's daughter, you'd be able to see her tits," said Adi with a laugh.

"Have you seen her before?" Dolah Supik asked.

"Yes."

"How was it? Did she bathe in the nude?"

"Of course she was nude!" Adi laughed again.

"No wonder you like to climb the banyan tree!" teased Dolah Supik. He then stared at the well for a long time without blinking. Only half of the floor of the well area was visible from where they were perched in the branches. Once in a while, Dolah Supik would shift his focus onto the three-in-a-row latrines. So far no one had come to pass motion or bathe at the well.

"How did Habsah's husband beat Abang Dolah up?" asked Dolah Supik, his eyes still focused on the well.

"He was stocky. He threw out a punch and Abang Dolah's nose bled," replied Adi excitedly.

"Why didn't Abang Dolah use his black magic?"

"He used the rod barring the door. He had no time to use his black magic."

"How did Kak Habsah fall for a man like Abang Dolah? He's not that handsome. And he's very thin! Kak Habsah is quite pretty, and her body is voluptuous."

"I believe tonight Kak Habsah's husband will come with his Lorong 21 gang members," said Adi.

"Mail Sengau will be there! Daud Cina will be there! Abang Yusoff will be there!"

"What if Kak Habsah's husband brings thirty men?" asked Adi.

"Someone is bathing!" Dolah Supik said, and Adi looked in the direction of the roofless well cubicle.

"Damn it! It's Mama Sulaiman bathing!" Adi laughed boisterously.

"What the hell!" said Dolah Supik, growling and cursing, and then spitting onto a branch of the banyan tree. Adi was still laughing. He then pointed at the bottom of the banyan tree and gestured to Dolah Supik to take a look.

"The spirit of this banyan tree lives inside the hole down there," Adi said, trying to frighten Dolah Supik. "It's a snake."

"To hell with it! I don't believe in it!" said Dolah Supik.

By the time they climbed down the tree, it was almost dusk. They had gobbled up the entire comb of golden bananas. When Adi entered his house along with Dolah Supik, they saw Kak Habsah talking to Mak Timah. Pak Mat was there too. Lately Pak Mat hardly stayed away from home. He was rarely seen anymore playing poker at the sarabat stall under the angsana tree. Mak Timah was happy at the changes in her husband's behaviour. But Pak Mat was getting thinner; his diabetes had started to gnaw at his bones.

"You must not go anywhere tonight," Pak Mat ordered. "Don't go to Abang Dolah's house." Adi nodded. He then said to himself, "While people are busy watching the attack by the members of Lorong 21, I will just join in."

Dolah Supik sat on the ambin with Adi. Kak Habsah helped Mak Timah to clean anchovies. Kak Habsah obviously looked worried. She knitted her brows each time she tore at the anchovies and started to imagine what would occur later in the night. "What a coward," she muttered to herself. She had been married to the stocky Omar for ten years. But he was fated to be impotent. Omar never talked nicely to her. Despite his thin body, Abang Dolah was able to provide her with physical satisfaction. She was attracted to Abang Dolah's manliness. He was highly skilled at black magic. She could never forget her sweet moments with Abang Dolah. Her healthy body and always-high libido indeed needed a man like Abang Dolah. Abang Dolah might be a poor man, yet she found him very sexually attractive.

• • •

The dusk sky was a purplish-red. The evening seemed to anticipate the events that might unfold later. No wind was blowing and the leaves of the banyan tree were stiff, the hanging roots still and straight. Dolah Supik and Adi anxiously waited for night to descend. Kak Habsah was more anxious. She went to the toilet every few minutes, unable to control her bladder, and then sat down again on the ambin. Mak Timah understood her anxiety. Pak Mat smoked one cigarette after another.

That night, at Abang Dolah's house, he and his friends waited for Kak Habsah's husband. Daud Cina hid a parang behind the door. Mail Sengau placed a metal pipe on top of the roof. Abang Yusoff hid a kris next to the well. Abang Dolah appeared calm as he waited for his enemy.

Pak Mat waited for the news of the arrival of the Lorong 21 gang. They waited until midnight. However, Kak Habsah's husband did not show up. Dolah Supik was bored and decided to go home. Abang Dolah asked Daud Cina, Mail Sengau and Abang Yusoff to also go home. But, they were reluctant. They waited until three in the morning; they were afraid that Kak Habsah's husband and his gang would attack in the wee hours. But still, even by four o'clock in the morning, the group from Lorong 21 had not turned up. So, Abang Dolah's friends went home. Kak Habsah returned to Abang Dolah's room. Adi had grown tired of waiting long ago, and had fallen asleep.

By dawn nothing had happened. The gang from Lorong 21 did not attack.

The days passed. Adi had already forgotten about Kak Habsah's husband. But eventually, once Abang Dolah was no longer expecting it, a gang from Lorong 21 beat him up at the crossroads near Lorong 25. His skull was fractured. Yet, he survived. The police investigated the case and

Kak Habsah's husband was arrested. When Abang Dolah returned home from the hospital, Kak Habsah began to live with him. They could not get married as Kak Habsah's husband refused to divorce her.

Eventually people began to forget about Kak Habsah and Abang Dolah's affair. Everything went on as normal. The banyan tree stood tall. Its yellowing leaves began to fall and lay scattered around Adi's house. In the evenings, thousands of starlings flocked to the tree, making a lot of noise. Adi continued to climb the banyan tree as he always had. Abang Dolah and Kak Habsah lived as husband and wife, even though their union was not solemnised.

AFFECTED BY
A LOKTANG

KAK SALMAH LOOKED at her face in the mirror. She fluffed up her hair. Her gold-inlaid tooth enhanced her sweetness when she smiled. She was dressed in a sarong that came up to her chest. As she raised her hand, her underarm looked smooth and fleshy. She lit a Triple Five cigarette and took a deep puff. She looked at her face again. "I'm still pretty," she whispered to herself.

Jamilah was doing the laundry. Kak Salmah had never known her real parents. Her foster mother had been as fierce as a lion, as well as a drunkard and an avid mahjong player. Kak Salmah's foster father had also been a drunkard and a wife-beater. Whenever her foster mother lost at gambling, her foster father would beat her up until she was half-dead.

At the age of fourteen, her drunk foster father raped her. Her foster mother had not been at home when it happened. That was the first time Kak Salmah experienced the pain of being raped, and she firmly kept the incident a secret. Not even her foster mother knew about it. But ever since the incident, she had developed a strong repulsion and hatred towards men. To her, all men were beasts, and beasts were violent and heartless. Kak Salmah recalled how her foster father had once gone sailing and never returned. It had been decades since she had last seen him.

"Jamilah! Come!" Kak Salmah called out. Jamilah rose from where she was doing her laundry and approached Kak Salmah nervously. "Massage me," Kak Salmah ordered.

Jamilah cautiously began to massage Kak Salmah. As she was about to pick up the Axe oil, the bottle slipped out of her hand. The medicated oil spilt onto the floor. Kak Salmah charged at Jamilah, seeing her foster mother's face in Jamilah's face. She pulled Jamilah's hair and pushed her to the floor. Kak Salmah hit and kicked Jamilah, who cried out loudly. Kak Salmah's madness became worse as she got increasingly furious. She was no longer herself. She picked up an empty stout bottle and swung it at Jamilah's head. Jamilah's shouts echoed throughout the barrack house. Several Chinese neighbours looked in the door to Kak Salmah's house. Kak Salmah moved towards the kettle on the stove. The water in it was still quite hot. Her foster mother's face seemed to be taunting her. She lifted the kettle and dumped the water over Jamilah's body. Jamilah cried out like a pig being slaughtered.

Kak Salmah noticed that her barrack neighbours had crowded in front of her door, and swore at them in Hokkien and Hainanese. She continued swearing as she locked the door. Jamilah groaned on the floor. Only then, as though waking, did Kak Salmah come out of her madness. She asked Jamilah to sit up and took off her dress. Jamilah's skin from her chest to her thighs was red and swollen. The bleeding on her head had stopped. Kak Salmah told Jamilah to wash her face. She then put some talcum powder on Jamilah's face. She covered Jamilah's swollen skin with lots of powder and told her to lie down and rest.

Kak Salmah sat on a stool. She lit up one of her Triple Five cigarettes. She sucked in deeply and blew out the smoke. Her Eurasian lover had not come home. She waited for him to return.

There was a knock at the door. Kak Salmah leapt up and opened it. It was Berahim Botak, who owned a provision shop near Kak Salmah's barrack. With him were two policemen.

"We received a complaint that you have been abusing your child," said one of the policemen. He looked Chinese.

"No, I didn't do so, who beat my child up?"

"Where is your child? We want to take a look," the policemen ordered. Both policemen were still standing at the doorway. Kak Salmah brought Jamilah outside. On seeing Jamilah, with powder on her face and no visible signs of injury, the policemen were forced to leave them alone. Several residents of the barrack house went behind the policemen and Berahim Botak. When the policemen had left, Kak Salmah blew her top. She swore again in Hokkien, directing her abuses at Berahim Botak. She was sure that he was the one who had reported her to the police. Kak Salmah opened two bottles of her stout, then gulped down samshu from her gripe water bottle. As she drank it, she yelled and swore at Berahim Botak in Hokkien. Her voice was very loud and was heard throughout the barrack house.

Kak Salmah ended up in front of Berahim Botak's shop. There was a big crowd outside the shop, which looked gloomy by the dim light from his pressure lamp. The money tin was hanging on a string above a glass cigarette showcase. Berahim Botak sat behind the counter and did not dare to come out. Kak Salmah swiftly ran inside, grabbed a nearby Pepsi Cola bottle and smashed it over his head, shattering the glass. Blood covered his face. More people gathered to witness the spectacle. An ambulance arrived and Berahim Botak was rushed to the hospital. The police handcuffed Kak Salmah and took her away in their patrol car, still raving.

Adi heard the news of Kak Salmah's arrest after she had been brought to the police station. Jamilah was alone and was crying in her house. That night, Jamilah was sent to a welfare home. Kak Salmah was released to await her trial date, but Jamilah was no longer allowed in Kak Salmah's care. By the time Kak Salmah returned from the police station the next morning, her lover, the macho Eurasian with tattoos on his body, had come home.

Kak Salmah drank more samshu. She drank more stout. And then a big fight occurred between Kak Salmah and her lover, ending with her stabbing her lover with a pair of scissors. He died three days later in the hospital.

This time around, Kak Salmah was arrested and kept in custody. The barrack area was quiet without her cursing and swearing. Berahim Botak, who had needed stitches from his injuries, felt at ease. Adi walked past Kak Salmah's house and noticed the door was shut. After that, for a long time Adi did not hear any more stories about Kak Salmah, although her face often appeared in Adi's mind, along with Jamilah's bruised and disfigured face.

Whenever Adi climbed the banyan tree, he thought about the fate of Kak Salmah. She had been sentenced to the gallows on a date that was yet to be determined. Adi overheard the conversations among the women in the village when they scolded their young daughters. Don't be a loose woman like Kak Salmah, they would say.

• • •

Adi heard from Mak Timah that his sister, who was living at Kolam Ayer Lane, had given birth to a daughter. Adi was now an uncle. Abang Dolah and Kak Habsah lived as husband and wife. Abang Dolah remained a member of the Norjawan band. Pak Mat had grown even thinner, and prayed regularly in a group at the surau. Even at home, Adi often saw his father praying. Pak Mat's diabetes had worsened; his arm was now numb and he could not feel his injections.

Adi's next-door neighbour, Tong San, had given birth to another child. His wife would tie the baby on to her back with a red sash, as she cleaned pork. The child's head would droop backwards. Bibik often dropped by Adi's house to see Pungut. It was now obvious that Pungut had been born that way because she had been affected by a loktang. Of late, Pungut had been shaking her head more aggressively and making the mosquito-like sound in a louder voice. Mak Timah kept on praying that Pungut would grow up like other normal children. Bibik was quite saddened by her granddaughter's fate. Busuk never dropped by to see her daughter. Pungut's father also never came to see her, nor did her siblings. Bibik alone bothered to come see her. Abang Dolah would often ask Pungut to pick some numbers for chap ji kee or four-digit lottery by scattering them before her, but he never won anything.

DEMONSTRATIONS

WHEN ADI AND his friend Dolah Supik arrived at the Chinese school the following week, they found many students preparing to walk out in a procession. Each student had a placard, inscribed with Chinese characters, in their hands. It had been several days since the students had begun to boycott their classes. They had gathered in the school compound and remained there; their parents brought them their meals, and showed anxiety and fear on their faces when they left the school compound. Outside the school, posted all around the school compound, police officers kept a watchful eye. Adi noticed that these policemen were no ordinary cops; they had helmets and carried shields and truncheons. Many students of the Chinese High School had gathered and formed a line. Their leader, a student with curly hair, was giving instructions.

Adi had earlier heard news that students of the Chinese school had launched a demonstration. But at that time, they had not dared go out on the streets. They had only gathered in the school compound and held their demonstration there. In the current crowd of students, Adi noticed the coconut-husk peeler's son. The pink-faced young man appeared enthusiastic about joining his friends in boycotting their classes, and he was carrying a red banner inscribed with some Chinese characters in white paint. The students were shouting at the policemen. Later they sang some Chinese songs. Their voices echoed down Tanjong Katong Road. A huge crowd watched their activities from outside the school. Adi imagined that if the students surged forward, the police would not be able to contain them; there were fewer than twenty policemen, compared to the more than five hundred students. The students continued singing. Once in a while, they would shout out in unison. Adi could not understand what they were shouting and singing about because it was all done in Chinese.

The coconut-husk peeler's son tried to provoke the policemen by pretending to lunge at them. He then went back inside the compound and joined his friends. Adi had heard from Abang Dolah that the Chinese students were demanding that the British government acknowledge the importance of Chinese education and use Chinese as an official language. The group inside the school was getting bigger. They formed several rows. The coconut-husk peeler's son appeared to be the busiest. He was giving out instructions. They seemed to be ready to storm out. Adi and Dolah Supik anticipated that something spectacular was about to happen. The students were now very close to the school fence. The police prepared to face them. And then, the students stormed out.

The police tried to stop them, but in vain. The students forced their way out onto the streets, moving about while shouting in Chinese. The policemen tried to beat them up with their truncheons. The students retaliated by crowding around the policemen. When finally the students dispersed, several policemen were sprawled on the road. Many students too were injured on their heads. The female students came forward to help and treat their male counterparts.

The students continued to march on, towards Geylang Road. Adi and Dolah Supik followed them. As they reached Queen Theatre, they became even more aggressive. They managed to flip over a car and then set it aflame. All the while, the shouting went on. Several police cars arrived. Many policemen streamed out of the cars, armed with truncheons and safety helmets. A clash ensued. The students were forced to disperse by the police. They scampered away into back lanes, chased by the police.

A gunshot was heard. Adi saw the coconut-husk peeler's son collapse. His friends helped lift him up. He appeared to have been shot in the stomach. The students carried him and continued in a procession along Geylang Road. The police stepped back. Many Chinese people gathered, looking angry. They hurled abuses at the police. The coconut-husk peeler's son was in severe pain. His head was drooping. The procession was now in front of Happy World amusement park, just ahead of the Lorong 3 crossroads, and an awed Adi and Dolah Supik followed behind. Adi noticed the coconut-husk peeler's son was no longer moving. His friends placed him down on the road and took him onto their laps. They screamed and yelled, taunting the police. When the police came at them, some of them scampered away. The coconut-husk peeler's son lay sprawled on the road. An ambulance arrived and carried him to the hospital. The police were now coming in droves. The students were gradually dispersed, many of whom had bleeding heads. Groups of students were escorted into police trucks and transported to the police station. About an hour later, the situation returned to normal. There was not even a single student on the road. The crowd had also gone home. Adi rode pillion on Dolah Supik's bicycle and went back to Kampung Pak Buyung.

The following day, the situation became worse. Other students of the Chinese school conducted a demonstration. Pak Mat prohibited Adi from leaving his house. He was not allowed to go see the demonstrations. He spent his time climbing the banyan tree and listening to stories from Abang Dolah at night. Abang Dolah told him that bus drivers and workers too had held demonstrations. The situation had worsened. A policeman had been killed, burnt alive by the protestors. Many buses also had been toppled over and set alight. It was very chaotic. Secret societies took advantage of the situation to rob and kill. The police seemed unable to control the situation. Many Gurkha policemen were brought in to keep the peace. Adi listened attentively to Abang Dolah's reports.

"This was all instigated by the Communists," said Abang Dolah, as he took a puff of his cigarette. "They want to topple the government by way of riots and then they will seize power." Adi kept quiet and dared not say a thing about having watched the procession the previous day. He was afraid of being scolded by Mak Timah.

The dead body of the coconut-husk peeler's son was brought home. The police guarded the coconut-husk peeler's house closely. The coconut-husk peeler cried until his eyes were swollen. For several days, the sound of Chinese praying and singing broke the silence around Adi's house. When the boy's corpse was taken to the cemetery, again many policemen accompanied it.

According to Abang Dolah, a reporter from America had also been killed. Students of the Chinese school had destroyed dozens of lorries near City Hall. They had covered their faces with handkerchiefs and gone on a rampage.

"The Communists influenced these immature youngsters!" said Abang Dolah. Adi did not quite understand the word "Communist". He imagined them to be evil and fierce. Abang Dolah had said the Communists did not believe in Allah. Adi was afraid when he heard this.

NOT SOMEBODY'S POODLE

BY THE TIME Pak Mat and Adi arrived at Market Street, it was already evening. There were still many passersby on the street, and the area was very busy. On their way there, they had walked by the Singapore River, which had been full of Chinese tongkangs. Several elderly Chinese men were carrying gunny sacks from the tongkangs to load them on to lorries. Pak Mat brought Adi to a house that had dried leaves hung across its doorway. Adi could smell the aroma of Indian incense.

"This is the chetty's place," said Pak Mat.

Pak Mat entered. A large Indian man dressed in a dazzling white sarong welcomed him. The chetty had a paunch, made more noticeable by the fact that he was not wearing a shirt. White ash was smeared on his forehead, with a red dot in the middle. There were about ten chettiars inside the house, sitting in two groups of five. On the ambin lay a mat and a wooden chest.

"How are you?" asked the chetty who had received Pak Mat. "It's been a long time since you last visited."

"I want to borrow some money, only fifty dollars. I need to buy books, a school uniform and shoes," replied

Pak Mat, his eyes to the floor.

"How to help you? You have yet to settle your past debts, and now you want to borrow some more? Tell me how." The chetty stared at Adi and sighed loudly. "I can only loan you twenty dollars, not more than that."

Pak Mat nodded.

"If you're no longer around, who will repay what you owe?"

"My son will be around," Pak Mat said, placing a hand on Adi's shoulder. "He will repay the loan, you need not worry."

The chetty took some money out from his wooden chest and then scribbled something in his notebook. "Don't forget to pay at the end of the month. If you can't reimburse the principal, you must at least pay the interest."

Adi would now be able to replace his worn-out shoes, as well as buy a pair of trousers and a shirt. He was happy. Pak Mat no longer used the money he borrowed from the chetty to gamble.

Later, as they were heading back home, Adi asked, "Have you borrowed a lot from the chetty?"

"One hundred and fifty dollars," replied Pak Mat. "But the interest grows every month."

"How much is the interest?"

"For every ten dollars, two dollars per month." Pak Mat sighed wearily.

"What? In that case, our debts will never be settled!" Adi yelped.

"If I'm dead, you must start working to continue to pay back my debts."

Pak Mat seemed to have left Adi with a bequest. Adi felt quite sad to hear his father talk about death. He looked at his father's figure as they walked along the road. Pak Mat was very thin. His long-sleeved shirt appeared too big for him, particularly since he had not tucked it in. He walked with a limp and would stop every once in a while, exhausted, to catch his breath.

His father's diabetes had ravaged him mercilessly. Every night, Pak Mat would ask his mother to massage his body, grimacing as he endured the pain in his bones. Adi would also massage his father's calves with ointment. He felt sad on thinking that his father would die while he was still in school.

He thought of the poverty that his father had endured all these years. His father's slippers were worn out and dirty and he had not bought new shirts in a long time. Looking at his father, Adi recalled Abang Dolah's words: When the Japanese had surrendered in 1945, every citizen in Singapore had been overjoyed. The people had happily welcomed back the British and the entire country had been in a festive mood. Cheers and music had hailed the return of the British army. When the Union Jack was raised again in front of City Hall, many people had felt grateful. Many had cried. The citizens had thought that the British would bring wealth to their country. But when Adi looked at his life and his father's sufferings less than two decades later, he felt miserable. Although the Japanese had left and the British were ruling again, the lifestyle of the people had not changed much. His family, and many others, were still poor.

As they reached a sarabat stall on the bank of the Singapore River, Pak Mat invited Adi to sit down. Pak Mat ordered a cup of tea with milk, and a bottle of Coca-Cola. Adi ate a piece of sweet cake. Pak Mat looked down as he sipped his tea with milk. Adi stared at his father's face. His father's beard was unkempt and untrimmed. Adi thought of his father's debts to the chetty, which he would have to settle upon his father's death. Adi fantasised that it would be so wonderful if only he were a prince, like in the old Malay tales that he had read. His father would not have to work so hard. His food and health would be taken care of, and he would live happily in a palace with a garden. When his father passed away, Adi would then succeed him. The life of a king, with his concubines, would indeed be enjoyable. Anytime he wished, he could bathe in a pool filled with lotus flowers, and pick from baskets full of grapes. How lucky I would be if my father were a king, Adi thought, smiling as he daydreamed.

Adi pictured Kak Salmah's face, thinking of how her life had also been full of hardships. She had been forced to live as a hustler, seeking solace in samshu and beer. As a result, Jamilah had had to suffer day and night. He pictured Abang Dolah, who had passed his Senior Cambridge exams, yet refused to work and lived in with

Kak Habsah. Adi pictured Dolah Supik's face, as he was pushing his drums. He visualised his mother's face as she cleaned Pungut's waste. His patient and resilient mother. Adi recalled the faces of his friends in school, faces that were weak and listless, figures that were thin and lazy. What kind of job would any of them get upon leaving school? Adi was certain that a seventh-grade graduate, especially from a Malay school, would never become an engineer, and was even less likely to ever become a government minister.

Adi came out of his daydream when Pak Mat asked if he was ready to leave the sarabat stall. Adi walked behind his father. They climbed a staircase next to a bridge and crossed the road to wait for a bus that would take them to Lorong 23. When he sat next to his father on the bus, Adi could feel his father's shoulder blade jutting out to rub against his arm. Pak Mat dozed off as the bus moved jerkily towards Geylang Road.

They alighted at the entrance to Lorong 23, which was teeming with Chinese hawkers selling all sorts of food. Not far away, in an empty field next to a paint shop, stood a grand stage for Chinese opera. The actors were busy putting on make-up behind the stage. Below the stage stood several foosball tables, with many people crowding around. Two children poked coconut frond sticks through the cracks on the floor of the stage.

The pressure lamps at the stalls that had been temporarily set up for the opera were yet to be lit. The hawkers were busy preparing their wares. The majority were Chinese stalls selling sweet-and-sour or pickled fruits. Adi salivated when he saw the pickled mangoes and papayas. As he was about to move on, he noticed Abang Dolah having a cup of coffee at Bopeng's shop. His neighbour was squatting on a round, dirty wooden stool, and waved over Pak Mat and Adi when he saw them.

"I'll go home, it's nearly nightfall," said his father. "I want to pray."

Adi left him and headed towards Bopeng's shop. Next to Abang Dolah were Mail Sengau and Daud Cina, all of them drinking thick black coffee. Their glasses were only half full, and fried peanuts lay scattered on the table. Adi entered and sat on a round stool next to Abang Dolah.

"Come with me to Kallang Airport to watch people campaigning," Abang Dolah told Adi. "They're putting up a petition for independence." He then added, "Would you like a drink? Bopeng, a cup of coffee please."

Bopeng returned with a cup of thick black coffee; its steam spiralled up into the air.

"Tonight, there will be many people, I guess thousands of them," Abang Dolah said. "You should come with me, hear them talk about independence."

Adi smiled. Daud Cina and Mail Sengau munched on fried peanuts. Adi looked again to the opera stage. Several elderly women were arranging seats in front, waiting for the play to begin. At the rear of the stage was a picture of a dragon with several flying fairies. To the left was a picture of a warrior brandishing a sword. On the right-hand side of the stage was a Chinese violin, ready for use.

While Adi was looking keenly at the decorations, the drapes suddenly closed. The intricate drapes were of a bright green colour and had shiny sequins at the bottom.

After Adi, Abang Dolah, Mail Sengau and Daud Cina all finished their coffees, they walked along Lorong 18 as the street lights came on. Several flying ants flew around the lamps. When they reached Kallang Airport, they found thousands of people already there, in a variety of ethnicities and odours. On the far end of the field was a stage, decorated with lights. The words *KAMI MAHU MERDEKA*—We Want Independence—were boldly printed on the screen at the back, and on the stage hung a banner inscribed with *MINGGU MERDEKA*—Independence Week.

"Tonight, they'll be collecting signatures of those who are in favour of independence," Abang Dolah explained. The crowd was now a sea of people. At about three hundred yards from the stage, Adi and the others had to stop; they could not get any closer, given the density of people in front of them. Some very important people would be giving speeches. Adi had never attended such a big gathering in his life.

The first speaker was someone who looked like a white man. He was greatly applauded by the sea of spectators below. When he screamed "Merdeka", everyone joined in. Adi shouted as well, as did Daud Cina and Mail Sengau, the latter in his nasal voice. Only Abang Dolah did not join in the cheering. The person spoke in English. Adi could not understand a thing.

"Who are you, to liberate our country?" Abang Dolah complained above the shouts. After the white man had spoken, it was the turn of a Malay man, who was wearing a songkok. The man was sturdy and had a chubby face.

"Merdeka!" the Malay man screamed.

"Merdekaaaaaa!" the sea of people echoed.

"Merdekaaa!" came another shout came from the stage.

"Merdekaaaaaa!" replied the sea of people below.

"Merdeka!" screamed the Malay man and he thrust his fists into the air.

"Merdekaaaaaa!" screamed the sea of people below as they raised their fists as well.

"United we stand, comrades! Remember, we don't want to stay very long under the armpits of the white men. We're not stupid. We're able to run our own country. Our group will be going to England to ask for independence. Comrades, support us! Leave your signatures! Let's seize independence!"

Abang Dolah pouted. He straightened his spectacles. He scratched his neck. It was very hot, given the huge crowd. Adi, Mail Sengau, Daud Cina and Abang Dolah were already drenched in their own sweat. Droplets of perspiration rolled down the sides of Adi's face.

"How to gain it?" Abang Dolah grumbled. "With a pen? The white men won't be so foolish! The white men aren't little kids!"

"Comrades, the Japanese have taught us that Asians can rule their own countries. The Japanese have shown us that they were able to conquer the white men! We are not demanding someone else's rights; we are asking for our own rights! Comrades, a colonised nation is a weak nation, a nation without integrity. A small and cowardly nation. We are not a stupid nation! My companions who stand beside me are not stupid people! They are lawyers and businessmen. They can talk, they can confront anyone. They even dare to face the king of the white men. So, do support us, comrades. Leave your signatures before our delegation goes to England to negotiate for independence."

"Whose country do you want to liberate?" Abang Dolah muttered under his breath again. "You foolish people! You collaborate with immigrants! Traitors!"

Daud Cina ran his fingers through his hair. Adi felt the heat, from the sea of people and from the Malay man's fiery words.

"Comrades, we have the right to determine our own destiny. We don't want to be somebody's poodle! Remember comrades, we're created equal by Allah. We're all humans with brains and minds. We're like the Japanese. We're like the Englishmen. We're like all human beings. They eat, we eat. They shit, we shit. Our blood is equally red. Our shit stinks equally. Comrades, remember, we must be ambitious! Be free-spirited! We have the right to rule our own country! Comrades, if we're united, unanimous, of one heart and soul, no one can defeat us. Not a single power can colonise us. This country is our country, our homeland. We must defend it. We must rule it ourselves! We don't want senseless bloodshed to occur. We want peace. Remember comrades, support us! Leave your signatures, comrades, in support of the petition for independence. Remember, independence means restoring the dignity of our race and country!"

Despite the speaker's impassioned words, Abang Dolah was still pouting. He was scratching his neck more vigorously. It was getting hotter and the crowd now smelled like sheep in a cage. The moon was getting brighter in the sky. The stars were twinkling.

"Who will be the ones liberated? You shall see, idiots!" Abang Dolah said sarcastically. Adi did not understand why Abang Dolah disagreed with the Malay man's words and was angry at him. He did not understand why Abang Dolah called the man a traitor.

Before the man in the songkok ended his speech, he cried out: "Merdeka!"

"Merdekaaaaaa!" the audience echoed, and the call-and-response continued several more times.

Next, a bespectacled Chinese man with short hair took his turn. He spoke for a long time. He also shouted "Merdeka!" thrice before and after his speech. Once again, the sea of people below echoed the chant. Then, a fat Indian man spoke and repeated the pattern.

When Adi, Abang Dolah, Mail Sengau and Daud Cina

left the mass rally that night, the moon had descended in the sky. The stars appeared lacklustre. Adi and his companions walked back through Lorong 18 and then entered Lorong 23. The Chinese opera in front of Lorong 23 was still playing when they reached the crossroads there. The stalls selling sweet-and-sour or pickled fruits were still brightly lit. The atmosphere appeared livelier. The voices of the opera actors cut through the late night.

"Our people don't understand the meaning of independence," Abang Dolah said as he walked along. "Independence is sacred! Independence is a noble obligation! You just see later, who will be liberated and who will be the coloniser!"

Adi, Daud Cina and Mail Sengau remained quiet as they listened to Abang Dolah's complaints. "Our people have yet to learn about politics, they have no political awareness, they let outsiders determine the integrity of our race, the integrity of their own country. People shout merdeka, they shout merdeka back. Like a parrot! Like a donkey! In the past, when the Japanese entered to occupy this country, the people gave them their support, hoping that the Japanese would give them riches, provide them with wealth! When the Japanese started to rape their maidens, only then they realised that they were as bad as the British! When the Japanese asked them to worship the sun, our Islamic scholars became cowards and worshipped the sun. Later, after independence, when they are ruled by the immigrants, only then will they know the antics and ruses of the infidel race."

That night, Adi did not sleep well. In his head, he kept hearing the audience's shouts and Abang Dolah's ravings. He was quite confused as he thought about independence and the people who wanted it. Earlier, when he had reached home, he had noticed that Tong Samboo's house was still brightly lit and there were many people outside; perhaps her half-insane daughter had committed suicide, but Adi could not know for sure. The banyan tree was enveloped in darkness; even the bright light of the moon could not cut through the dense and overlapping leaves.

As Adi lay down on the mengkuang mat, a song from Ah Kong's Rediffusion was faintly audible. Pak Mat coughed continuously. Mak Timah nagged at him for smoking too much. Pungut was already fast asleep. She looked just like her mother, with her slit-like eyes, small mouth and sparse hair. Adi remembered what Bibik had said about Pungut being an unlucky child. Pungut would not bring good luck to her guardians. She would bring hardship. Adi turned away to look at the walls of the house with their cracks and small slits. The cracks, it seemed to him, were in the shape of a monitor lizard. There were also snake-like figures on the wall. Adi gazed at the ceiling. The colour was sad and grim. Several layers of rubber matting and rusty tin had been fixed over the leaks. Adi noticed a fat lizard with its wiggly tail looking down at the floor of the room. Pak Mat was still coughing. He had a long and loud cough, shrill, like a dog's. He seemed to have gallons of phlegm stuck in his throat. Adi felt sad as he heard his father coughing. He recalled the face of the Indian chetty who had loaned money to his father.

A thousand and one thoughts haunted Adi's mind. He found it hard to close his eyes. He pictured the dark cavity of the banyan tree. He imagined the guardians of the banyan tree crawling out with their bulging eyes and protruding tongues to eat the eggs offered by the Chinese worshippers. He kept thinking about the various incidents of the day. The shouts of "Merdeka!" continued to ring in his ears.

SHOUT UNTIL
THE SKY FALLS

THE SCORCHING SUN shone down hard on Kota-Kota Malay School. It was an extraordinarily hot day. Steam shimmered off the surface of the road in front of the school. As usual, during his break, Adi bought a curry puff and went to sit under a cherry tree. None of the cherries on the tree were ripe; the students soon picked even the ones that had turned yellowish. Around ten Primary Seven students had gathered in front of the hall. A big-bodied, bespectacled student was speaking animatedly. Adi wanted to know what was being so seriously discussed, so he went nearer.

"Tomorrow, they will go on a strike," the large-bodied student was saying. He pushed the spectacles that had slid down his nose back up. "We must support them. This is a question of our future."

"What preparations must we make?" asked another student.

"We need not do anything. They have prepared everything. Our job is only to join the crowd," the first student replied. It did not take much for Adi to understand that the students were planning to join in a strike. What he did not know, however, was who would be going on strike. "We carry placards, and shout in support," added the student. His other friends nodded.

"We must shout loudly," said a very petite student.

"We shout until the sky falls," added another.

"Until the sky falls," the burly student reaffirmed. "But remember, this is a secret. Don't let outsiders know. Don't let the police know. Don't let our teachers know." He adjusted his spectacles again.

Adi thought of the previous demonstration by the Chinese school students, and how they had clashed with the police. Would these students too end up clashing with the police, tomorrow?

The burly student's next words answered his question. "Remember, we're going to hold a peaceful strike. Don't cause trouble. Don't go out of the school compound. We don't want any bloodshed. We're not violent. We're not animals. We're just holding a demonstration to show our unhappiness. We only want to present our demands, demands that are not being heard by the white men. That's all.

"But the possibility of violence is still there. It all depends on our actions. We must stay cool-headed and contain our anger. We will present our demands in a peaceful manner. Even if the police act rough with you, do not engage them. If violence is repaid with gentleness, nothing untoward will happen." All the other students concurred.

The bell rang, indicating the break was over. The burly student gave a final set of instructions. "Invite more of our friends, but remember, only those whom we can trust."

As all the students lined up in the hall after their break, they were not allowed to return to their classrooms. Instead, the principal was going to make a speech. The students were told to sit down on the floor of the main hall and instructed not to make any noise.

"You're still students," the principal said, standing at the front of the hall. "Your future depends on your good behaviour. Don't listen to the politicians and don't get involved in political affairs. Your duty is to study hard. The issue of whether or not you can get into a secondary school is not your problem. Leave the matter to the concerned people." He stared at the faces of the students before him. Adi and his schoolmates remained silent as they listened to what was undeniably a warning.

"If I find that any of you were involved in undesirable activities, anything that is against the school's regulations, you will be expelled," the principal intoned sternly. Adi was quite certain that the principal was referring to the next day's strike.

That evening, before Adi went home, a Primary Seven student spoke to him. "Tomorrow, meet at Geylang-Geylang. Get there by early morning!"

It was then clear to Adi that the Primary Seven students would not be going on strike in their school but at Geylang-Geylang. Adi was interested in the invitation. On his journey home, he kept visualising the event that would unfold tomorrow. He resolved to take part in the strike the next morning.

As Adi walked out from behind the Chinese barracks, he saw a loktang dancing in front of Tong Samboo's house. The man was in his thirties, and his tongue protruded from his mouth; a sharp metal rod pierced through his tongue, but there appeared to be no blood. The loktang's body was covered all over with tattoos. He stood firm on his right foot, and danced by means of crossing his left foot over the right, again and again. With him were several other people. Two boys were beating drums and an old man stood holding a long whip in his hand. The loktang then took the whip and began whipping himself with it. He then lashed at the door of Tong Samboo's house with it. Adi was certain that Tong Samboo had called in the loktang to get rid of a ghost in her house, or else she was using his services to treat her half-insane daughter. Adi sat on the ambin in front of his house and watched the loktang's antics. The loktang kept dancing at Tong Samboo's door for about half an hour. After that, he moved on to the banyan tree. The loktang's assistant planted a short bamboo pole with a red cloth tied to it, near the tree. He then stuck a piece of paper with Chinese characters on the bamboo pole. Adi figured that the loktang meant to appease the spirits of the banyan tree, whom he believed to be the cause of Tong Samboo's daughter's condition.

Eventually, Adi entered his house. He saw his father lying sick on the bed. Pak Mat was groaning and shivering despite the thick blanket Mak Timah had wrapped around his body.

"Adi, go to the shop to buy aspirin and Axe oil. Your father is sick," ordered Mak Timah. "And fill up the drinking water, there's not a single drop left."

Adi went to the bathroom, picked up the two kerosene tins and carried them to the communal tap. All the while, he worried about his father. Pak Mat's conversation with the chetty at Market Street also playing in his ears: *My son will be around. He will repay the loan, you need not worry.*

• • •

It was already dusk. The western sky still was reddish, though the sun had set a while ago. Thick clouds scudded across the sky. Several sparrows perched on electrical wires, sitting side by side in a long row. The street lamp in front of Bongkok's shop had been lit. The dim light from the street lamp evoked a sense of melancholy.

At the communal tap, five people were already waiting for their turn to fill water. Two Chinese women were doing their laundry. The communal pipe had two taps. The paint around the middle of the pipe had peeled off. The whitish ground by the taps had many indentations. The cemented area by the pipe extended all the way to a drain that carried away the dirty bath and laundry water. The two women who were washing their clothes were busy talking in Hokkien. When Adi's turn came, he quickly placed a kerosene tin under the tap. It did not take long for the water to flow over. Soon, the other tin was also filled up to the brim. Adi then carried them home. The veins on his arms stood out under their weight. As he walked, water spilled from the tins, wetting his pants and legs. By the time he reached home, only three-quarters of the tin would be full. It would take Adi three trips back and forth from the communal tap to fill up the jar of drinking water in his house. By his third trip back home with the water, hundreds of starlings were swarming around the banyan tree in a cacophony of sound.

The aspirin, as well as a massage with Axe oil, seemed to bring some relief to Pak Mat. He was no longer shivering and was finally able to fall asleep. But every now and then, he would wake up and ask Mak Timah to massage his legs again. Sometimes Adi would take over from Mak Timah and massage his father's limbs. But Pak Mat did not quite like the way Adi massaged him and said it gave him no relief. He soon asked Mak Timah to do it instead, every time. His eyes had sunk into their sockets and no longer sparkled. His lips were dry. He refused to eat or drink anything and instead asked Adi to light up his cigarette. Whenever he smoked, Pak Mat would cough incessantly. At times, it lasted for nearly ten minutes. Pak Mat felt as if his chest would burst when he coughed. He brought up no phlegm, instead spitting out what looked like thick, slimy saliva. Pak Mat's face looked sallow and he stared long at Adi with an inscrutable gaze that seemed to hold much meaning. Likewise, when Pak Mat stared at Mak Timah, he seemed to be looking at something beyond her face.

Adi recalled the face of the pot-bellied Hindu chetty with a pottu on his forehead. He thought of his father's debts, which had accumulated over time like breeding piglets. One hundred and fifty dollars. For every ten dollars, the interest was two dollars. For one hundred, the interest was twenty dollars; add another loan of fifty dollars, the total interest would be thirty dollars. And, the interest would add up every month. Adi wondered how to settle his father's debts, once he had found a job, in the future.

That night Adi slept with a troubled mind. The face of the chetty at Market Street flashed in his mind, followed by the face of the burly, bespectacled student, and then the face of the loktang with his pierced tongue. His father's pallid face too, invaded his thoughts and his loud cough disturbed Adi's sleep. Adi dreamt that he heard people shouting, demanding a secondary school. The faces swarmed his mind once again, flashing one after the other, in front of his eyes.

FATHER PASSES AWAY

GEYLANG-GEYLANG SCHOOL was already full of with students, most of them girls. On the wire fence hung a big banner proclaiming: WE WANT A MALAY SECONDARY SCHOOL.

Each of the girls held a small placard with a slogan on it. Students gathered at the school canteen, at the place where chairs and tables were cleaned. In all this chaos, Adi remembered his mother's caution to not wander about since his father was critically ill. But he had been adamant about joining the strike at Geylang-Geylang. Without his mother's knowledge, he'd run from Lorong 23 to Geylang-Geylang.

A bespectacled Chinese-looking man made a speech in Malay. "We are entitled to study to whatever level we want. No one can stop us. We don't want to remain labourers and policemen forever. Our demands are legal. The colonisers have been deliberately oppressing us. They don't want us to become clever. The white men's government deliberately wants us to remain stupid forever, so that they will find it easy to rule us. We want Malay secondary schools to be built urgently. We don't want to become gardeners like our fathers. We don't want to become labourers like our grandfathers. We want to study further. We want to be well-educated."

All the students applauded after hearing his speech.

"We make a sacrifice today for the future. Even if we don't succeed, our younger siblings and our children will. We can't just cross our arms and do nothing. We can't just surrender to fate. We must change things. We shouldn't be afraid of the colonisers' threats and retaliation. We must make sacrifices for our own future. The colonisers have been ruling us for so long. We are being colonised in all aspects. Our minds are being colonised. Our souls are being colonised. Our culture is being colonised. Others are determining our future. How much longer will we act like a buffalo pulled around by its nose? Until Judgement Day? Until another World War?"

The man spoke with great passion. The students began to shout and curse the colonisers: The white men can go back to their own country! Their shouts reverberated through the air and everyone became very spirited. They raised their placards high. Several newspaper journalists had arrived. Photos were taken in quick succession. After the first man had spoken, an old, bespectacled man in long-sleeved shirt and a songkok, with neatly-combed hair, began to speak.

"With just a Primary Seven education, where else can you all go? It's true that there are students who furthered their studies in English schools, but how many of you will make it there? What about the rest? The rest drop out like dry litter, and lie scattered in dirty drains. The rest become dust on the streets. They become tramps. They become trishaw pedallers. They become labourers to big bosses. They remain guards until they die. They become drivers for pot-bellied men. Are you willing to let that happen to you?"

The students answered the old man's questions with shouts and curses against the colonisers, the white men. The old man continued in a fiery tone.

"Remember, our race is great! We are spread out throughout the archipelago! Our culture is advanced! We feel small because we're colonised. The white men have belittled and demoralised us. We deem ourselves, our culture, and our education as useless because of their brainwashing. That's the politics of the colonisers. That's the reason the white men don't want us to study at higher levels, so that all of you will remain stupid! So that all of you will only know how to plant vegetables and rear goats and ducks! So that all of you will only know how to make waste-paper baskets!

"Today, we rise up. We demand that the government build secondary schools. We want to see the day when you will get to study until university. That is our demand!"

Some policemen had barricaded the areas outside the school. A loudspeaker boomed orders for the students to disperse. Before Adi left the compound of Geylang-Geylang School, he spotted the man who had spoken first, the old man in the songkok, and several others being hustled into a police vehicle. And then, the situation quickly returned to normal. Geylang-Geylang was quiet.

• • •

Adi hastened home. His mother's words banged hard on his eardrums. He walked along Lorong 21 past the houses on stilts and entered Lorong 21A, then went directly through Lorong 23.

When Adi arrived home, Abang Dolah and Kak Habsah were present. Mail Sengau was also there. Pak Mat's illness had gotten worse. Mak Timah's eyes were red from crying. According to Abang Dolah, Pak Mat had passed out twice. Adi approached his father and tried to wake him up. His father opened his eyes, but only for a moment. He gave Adi a blank stare and then closed his eyes again. Adi was overcome with sadness, and he cried as he sat next to his father and massaged his legs. His father did not open his eyes. Abang Dolah asked for a bowl of water and recited some prayers. Then he brushed Pak Mat's face with his hand. Pak Mat still did not open his eyes.

That night Pak Mat finally opened his eyes and stared at the roof beam for a long time. He was mumbling something, but his words were unclear. His tongue was stiff. Mak Timah asked Mail Sengau to go find Adi's sister at Kolam Ayer Lane.

"I've heard that she lives behind the dhoby shop. Please look for her and ask her to come here immediately." Mail Sengau left immediately on his Raleigh bicycle.

As Pak Mat's illness worsened that night, Abang Dolah

began to read aloud the Yassin, chapter 36 of the Quran, which was often recited at funerals. Mak Timah continued to cry. Inside the room, Pungut obliviously shook her head and made her usual mosquito-like sound. Adi remained at his father's side. He felt sad that he could not read the Yassin properly like Abang Dolah did. Abang Dolah asked Adi to read the Fatihah and Qulhu, the first and 112th chapters of the Quran, as many times as possible. Adi then recited them in his heart continually. Pak Mat's eyes remained fixed on the roof beam. Every so often, Abang Dolah would whisper the chant "La ilaha illallah" into Pak Mat's ears: "There is no deity worthy of worship but God." Pak Mat seemed to follow Abang Dolah's recitation with his stiff tongue, although he was unable to speak.

At around eleven o'clock, Mail Sengau returned. With him were Adi's sister, her muscular, dark-skinned husband Omar, and their baby daughter. This was the first time Adi had seen his sister's pretty, sharp-nosed child. His niece.

Adi's sister cried and hugged Mak Timah. Then she moved to Pak Mat's side. Mak Timah asked her to put on a shawl and make her ablutions. Adi's sister then replaced Abang Dolah in reading the Yassin. Every now and then she would stop to wipe her tears. Pak Mat's eyes were still fixed on the beam of the roof. Adi continued to read the Fatihah and Qulhu.

Adi moved to the window. He looked out at the banyan tree. It was covered in darkness. The street lamp next to the coconut-husk peeler's house was dim and feeble. He somehow felt as though the banyan tree understood his pain and sadness.

Abang Dolah chanted "La ilaha illallah" more frequently into Pak Mat's ears. Pak Mat had stopped moving his lips, but when Abang Dolah finished whispering the chant, Pak Mat cleared his throat as if to indicate that he had been following it all along.

Adi's father breathed in deep a few times. Mak Timah, Adi's sister, his brother-in-law, Kak Habsah, Mail Sengau and Abang Dolah were all next to him. Adi stared into his father's face. Pak Mat appeared to be finding it harder to breathe. He grimaced as he endured the pain.

Then he stopped breathing.

Mak Timah cried loudly. So did Adi's sister. Abang Dolah asked Mak Timah for a batik cloth to cover Pak Mat's body. Kak Habsah struck a match, lit some pieces of charcoal and placed them in an incense burner. She then sprinkled some benzoin onto the burner. The whole room filled with the smell of vanilla. Abang Dolah then continued to read the Yassin. Adi's sister did the same. Adi read the Fatihah and Qulhu as he touched his father's legs. Adi noticed his father's legs had begun to turn cold. Once in a while Adi lifted the cloth that covered his father's face. He looked at his father's face for a long time before covering it again with the cloth. He felt painfully sad.

Mak Timah cried incessantly. Adi's sister wailed as she asked pardon from Pak Mat for her wrongdoings towards him. Kak Habsah consoled her. Mail Sengau had gone to inform the other residents of the kampung, and the imam of the surau, of Pak Mat's passing. Shortly after that, people came to pay their respects. They read the Yassin in turns. Adi and his sister remained seated next to their father's body. Pungut shook her head and made her sound. She did not know anything. She did not know that Pak Mat had passed away. She knew nothing at all.

Before daybreak, Adi was on his way to the toilet, when he saw Kak Habsah consoling his mother.

"Don't worry, sister. I have some jewellery. In the morning, ask Mail Sengau to pawn it. The pawnshop at Lorong 25 is not that far away. Take these bangles and necklace. Later, when you have the money, you can redeem them. Take them, sister." Mak Timah was reluctant to accept the gifts, but Pak Mat's body had to be set to rest. She needed money for the shroud, to pay the undertaker to wash the body, and to pay for the burial services and a memorial feast.

"Take them, sister. You have helped me and Abang Dolah greatly. Now it is my turn to help you out. Please take them!" Kak Habsah placed her bangles and necklace in Mak Timah's hands. Adi's mother burst into a fresh batch of tears. Kak Habsah consoled her again.

"We're poor folk, sister. Only we know each other's sufferings. It's all right. Stop worrying." Adi was moved upon seeing Kak Habsah's kindness.

"Tomorrow, early in the morning, ask someone to buy about forty packets of prata and some sugar, for those who will accompany the body to the burial ground," said Kak

Habsah. "Later, I'll go to the market to buy the things for a tahlil reception."

The voices of people reading the Yassin broke the silence of the early morning. Three to four men were sitting outside the house. Adi's sister remained next to Pak Mat's body. Her child was fast asleep next to Pungut. Once in a while, the sound of a woodpecker was heard coming from the banyan tree. Every now and then, Adi would lift up the veil over his father's face and gaze at it for a long time. Pak Mat's lips appeared to be indented on the right side, as if he had been biting his lips to endure the pain in the final moments before he had passed away. His eyes were shut tight and his scruffy beard and long moustache were stiff. Adi placed the veil back over his father's face and continued to recite the Fatihah and Qulhu as many times as he could.

• • •

The sun rose. Starlings chirped loudly at the break of dawn. The leaves and trunk of the banyan tree were wet with dew. Many residents of Kampung Pak Buyung had already gathered at Adi's house, and some were chatting under the banyan tree. At around nine o'clock in the morning, a newly-made casket was placed on two chairs, next to one of the windows. Bibik brought over her long rubber hose, which ran all the way from a tap in her kitchen to Adi's house. This was in order to wash Pak Mat's body. Tong San's children were afraid to come out. The Chinese villagers walked hurriedly past Adi's house. Abang Dolah looked tired. He had stayed awake all night long to read the Yassin. Adi's baby niece had woken up early in the morning and was now crying continuously. Pungut was still fast asleep. At ten o'clock in the morning, the person who had been called to wash the body arrived. Dolah Supik came bringing with him a stretcher for the coffin, as well as a green cloth with Jawi inscriptions on it. Adi saw Yunos Potek, Kassim Boca, and Dolah Supik. The Sikh from the sarabat stall also came. At eleven o'clock in the morning, about twenty of Pak Mat's colleagues arrived. They handed over an envelope of donation money to Mak Timah. She was touched and accepted it with gratitude. The women visitors stayed inside while the men would go out to sit under the banyan tree, after paying their respects to Pak Mat's body.

When Adi was about to sprinkle sandalwood dust over his father's body, he sobbed uncontrollably. His sister wailed and pleaded that her wrongdoings against Pak Mat be forgiven. Adi stared at his father's face for the last time. After he sprinkled the sandalwood, the body was ready to be brought to the Bidadari Cemetery. Before the body was taken outside, Abang Dolah made a speech asking those in attendance to consider as settled all food and drink that were consumed by Pak Mat. He also asked that they forgive Pak Mat for any transgressions during his lifetime. When the body was about to be taken out the door, Mak Timah wailed and lamented for her wrongdoings towards Pak Mat. Kak Habsah consoled her. With a final recitation of the Fatihah and with the proclamation, "Allahu Akbar," Pak Mat's body was carried to the surau for prayers.

The villagers of Kampung Pak Buyung took turns to carry the coffin. Many said their final prayers for Pak Mat. Those who did not join in the prayers sat under the bamboo trees beside the surau. Then the body was taken to the Bidadari Cemetery. The procession from Kampung Pak Buyung to the Bidadari Cemetery took less than half an hour. The young men of the kampung again took turns to carry the coffin. As they walked, they chanted the phrase "La ilaha illallah."

A few men helped lower the body into the grave. The strings of the shroud were untied. Pak Mat's body was covered with earth, and then the imam of the Kampung Pak Buyung surau read the funeral sermon. Everyone in attendance bowed their head. The sun was scorching, overhead. It felt as though the tombstones at the cemetery were standing tall and rigid. Adi was overwhelmed with grief on seeing his father's body for the last time. He let his tears fall, unrestrained.

• • •

That night, after a simple feast of bananas and fritters, Abang Dolah, Kak Habsah, Ani, and her husband were the only ones to remain. Adi's baby niece cried without pause. She quietened down after Abang Dolah gave her sanctified water, only to begin crying again, half an hour later. Adi's sister was thus forced to return with her child to Kolam Ayer Lane, even though she had planned to stay for the next three days. She promised to come back the next day and for the whole week thereafter. She would come by to keep the distraught Mak Timah company.

"You can come live with me, Ma," Adi's sister offered.

"Let me think about it," replied Mak Timah. She seemed to be lost deep in thought.

"If you stay with me, Omar can help monitor Adi in his studies. There's no one else to supervise him." Mak Timah did not reply. She remained silent.

After Adi's sister left, Abang Dolah and Kak Habsah stayed behind.

"Poor Pak Mat," Abang Dolah said. "He lived a hard life. He was a man of few words. He was never well-off, but he was kind-hearted. Pak Mat was the first person who invited me to rent a room here. I won't forget his kindness."

"I was often tired and so was gruff with him lately," Mak Timah said. "This is what makes me feel sad."

"Please, sister," Kak Habsah said. "Don't think too much on this. Pak Mat has certainly forgiven all that."

"The other night, he asked me to cook bean porridge, his favourite food. I did not do it. Pak Mat passed away in misery. Not only did I not make him the bean porridge he wanted, I scolded him instead!" Mak Timah sobbed again.

Kak Habsah and Abang Dolah went back home that night. Adi felt very lonely.

That night he lay down next to his mother and Pungut.

He had difficulty falling asleep. The image of his father being wrapped in a shroud, his indented lips, his sunken eyes, his pained breathing as he died: all these things appeared in Adi's mind. Only then did it dawn on him that he had lost the one person he relied on the most. Who would now provide for them? Who would pay for the house rent? Who would cover his school expenses? What if the chetty came to demand settlement of the loan? He wondered what it was like for his father to lie alone in the ground. He supposed it would be dark and frightening. How would his father reply to questions from Munkar and Nakir, the angels who appear after death to question one's deeds on earth? Only yesterday, his father had been with them. Human life was very short.

It was well into the night by the time Adi finally fell asleep. He dreamt that his father came to him, dressed in shabby clothes, his mouth bleeding, instructing him in a raspy voice to repay his loans to the chetty.

By the time Adi woke up, it was after dawn. Mak Timah had already woken up and was reading the Quran. The noisy cry of starlings filled the air. Adi planned to go out shortly; he wanted to plant a cananga tree on his father's grave. He hoped that the tree would grow to be healthy and produce thousands of flowers. Adi wanted to tell his father that he would pay off his debts once he started working.

Adi waited for the day to begin.

PART
2

IF THE TOWN OF MALACCA FALLS

THE MEETING WAS being held at Pak Ariff's house. Pak Ariff was the head of the goat's head logo party, a brawny man with a wide forehead and a neatly trimmed moustache. He wore a light blue batik shirt. Pak Ariff stuttered a bit as he spoke, especially when he was upset. Before him, on the plastic-covered wooden table, lay a heap of thick files. Twelve committee members of the goat's head logo party sat around the table on which coffee and fried banana fritters had been placed.

"The General Elections will be held soon. We must step up our campaign. We must now consider where to place our candidates." Pak Ariff paused to take a sip of his coffee. "How many candidates should we field?"

"Five," Abang Dolah said.

"Three," said a smartly-attired member.

"Ten. Three is too few. We should field ten," said another member, who sat next to Abang Dolah.

"We had better identify the areas where we have many supporters. We have to check our funds to see if it's sufficient or not to field our candidates," Pak Ariff said, stuttering slightly.

"Let's place a candidate in Geylang," said Abang Dolah.

"Kembangan," added another member.

"Southern Islands," the member next to Abang Dolah said again.

"Pasir Panjang, Siglap, Changi," added the smartly-attired man.

"We must avoid having a three-pronged fight," Pak Ariff said. "We must avoid contesting in places where the axe logo party is contesting. It would be a waste of time."

"In that case, it's hard to make any decision now," Abang Dolah said. "Let us wait until Nomination Day. We can only speculate at present. We can only roughly guess the areas where we can contest. Come Nomination Day, we will decide. Even at the last minute, there's nothing to lose. What's needed now is for us to identify the areas where we have a chance. If those areas are not contested yet, we can contest there."

Pak Ariff agreed with Abang Dolah, but he wanted to be sure that a full survey would be carried out immediately in the areas where the party had lots of supporters. The research, he said, was important to devise their strategy for the elections and to gain voters.

"Respected chairman, I would like to make a suggestion," said the party's secretary, a fierce, strict man. All eyes turned to him.

"I think our mission and that of the axe logo party are hardly different. We're both of the same stock. Our ambition and aspirations are the same. That is, to achieve independence and to defend our race. Isn't it detrimental for us to be disunited? How good it would be if we could all unite to fight against our common enemy, the white colonisers. The votes of our people wouldn't be divided and we would gain a good number of votes. We should discuss this with the axe logo party members. What do you think?"

Pak Ariff's eyes widened as he heard his secretary's words.

"Our mission is not the same," Pak Ariff said, clearly upset. "We have our own principles, our own ideology. We don't wish to collaborate with or hand over our political rights to the migrants. We don't intend to share power with them. We want the bumiputeras, the true 'sons of the soil', to rule this country. The axe logo party members are different—they intend to be tolerant towards the migrants. They intend to share political power with the migrants. This is where we differ from them." Pak Ariff glared at his secretary, and continued. "We don't like the feudal class. They like them and praise them. They're loyal and subservient to them. We fight for the rights of the people, for the people. We want the working class to hold power; we want to distribute wealth equally. There should be no authoritarian class. No feudal class. They, on the other hand, worship capitalists. That's the big difference between us and them." The committee members were all silent.

"We want a bigger state for the entire Malay archipelago, the Nusantara. We have been divided for too long, chopped to pieces. We have been slashed off like a tree branch. We want to join our biological siblings again. We oppose the separation imposed on us by the colonisers. We want the Nusantara flag to flutter all over the world. We want our language, the language that is spoken by hundreds of millions of people, to be recognised and respected, to be spoken at the UN. That is our manifesto. But not so with the axe logo party. They favour the migrants. We object to this. We object!" Pak Ariff's eyes were red and his lips quivered as he spoke. Nobody dared to interrupt his outburst. Everyone remained quiet and reflected on his words. The party's secretary nodded.

Pak Ariff continued. "If the secretary doesn't understand his party's manifesto, how can he act as its secretary? If the secretary doesn't know the ideological differences between the two parties, how can he be a secretary? Just consider the two members of the axe logo party, who have been sitting comfortably together at a table with the white men. What have they done? Did they fulfil their promises? When the students approached them to ask for a Malay secondary school, what did they say? 'What do we need a Malay secondary school for? Until what level do we want to study? What do we wish to be? The Malay language seems to clash with the white men's.' Hah! That's the answer. I regard them all as traitors! When they sit on comfortable chairs, rubbing shoulders with the white men, they forget their own race. Do you really want to tell me to unite with such people?

To merge our party with theirs?" Pak Ariff frowned. "They have never studied the history of how the 1874 treaty was made! They have no idea how the feudal class divided this country, how they wrestled with one another to seize wealth...to the extent that they were willing to be bought by the white men."

Abang Dolah added: "They have never understood how the Dutch and British divided us, how the damned white men severed us, how they partitioned the borders of our lands according to their wishes. One ruled this side. Another ruled that side." He stared directly at the secretary, studying him intently.

"Didn't you study the history of how Malacca fell? Don't you know how the foreigners toppled Malacca from within? What did the feudal class do when Malacca fell? The Portuguese did not colonise everything from Kedah up to Johor. They only captured a small area of the Malacca town. Had the feudal class been united they would have been able to defeat the Portuguese, but that was not the case. For hundreds of years after, we lived under the Portuguese. Do we look up to such people?"

The secretary finally spoke. "Not all members of the axe logo party agree to give political rights to the immigrants. Not all members of the party support the feudal class. Not all. Some oppose them. We should unite with just the opposing group!"

Pak Ariff could foresee dissent within the party. Some members had begun to feel inadequate and wanted support from other parties. If such matters were left unchecked, it would spell the collapse of the goat's head logo party. The party's strength would be lost.

"We must not forget who handed this island over to the white men!" Abang Dolah said. "For a little pension money, this island was sold! To satisfy the craving for opium and women, this island was handed over to the colonisers. Our mission to unite the states within the archipelago will be a success. Our lands will fall back into our hands. The enemies will leave and we will be reunited. People from across the border in Malaya have agreed to the proposal to unite under one flag, one race, one language. The people of the archipelago will speak a common language, Bahasa Nusantara. We're not small, we're great! We have hundreds of millions of members. Don't look inward, look outward, only then we will feel that we're not small. Our brothers are keen to help. They say: If the town of Malacca falls, they will rebuild it with planks from Java. Why then must we retreat, why must we surrender?"

The day's meeting was very heated, indeed as hot as the afternoon sun that fell on the zinc roof of Pak Ariff's house. Abang Dolah became very upset when the secretary then said: "If we wish to be elected by the people, we should behave properly. We should be righteous. We must serve as an example to others. We must be clean. Even if we are intelligent, if we lived like a tramp and refused to work, if we had a mistress, how will the people elect us? We only know how to talk big, but have skeletons in our closets."

Abang Dolah felt stung by the secretary's snide remarks. He knew that the secretary was referring to no one else but him. His heart burnt with rage. The acute pain from the secretary's remarks was akin to a rusty blade embedded in the core of his heart.

• • •

The evening was gloomy for Abang Dolah. The sky on the western horizon was red. Several swallows were flying low, once in a while diving until they almost touched the ground. Thick clouds moved as if chained together with sadness.

Abang Dolah walked home, his heart flaring with rage. He wanted to reach home quickly and think about how he could deal with the loud-mouthed secretary. He reached his room to find Kak Habsah lying down. She was clad in only a sarong tied just above her bosom. A packet of rice that she had bought earlier that day, at Lorong 7, lay on top of the milk carton. Abang Dolah did not even touch it. He sat on the ambin, thinking of ways to get back at the secretary of his party.

"I'm not working, but I don't go around begging for his father's assets. I don't work for the colonisers. And I'm still not dead of starvation," grumbled Abang Dolah. Kak Habsah approached him and tried to cuddle him. Abang Dolah rejected her advances by saying that he was tired and disturbed.

"Maybe he's a spy for the white men?" Kak Habsah suggested when Abang Dolah told her about the meeting.

"I don't know. He seems strange," explained Abang Dolah as he took off his white shirt. He also took off his singlet. His ribs and shoulder blades jutted out prominently.

"Had I been working for the white men, had I been a footstool for them, I would have become a minister by now! Bloody fool! He's not even educated, yet so eager to insult others."

Abang Dolah suddenly thought of Adi. Tomorrow he would ask Adi to look for worms from the smelliest carcass he could find. If possible, from a mouse or a pig. He wanted to cast a black magic spell against the secretary of the goat's head logo party. He would make the man's stomach bloat and cause his backside to be infested with worms until he had to pass motion and urinate lying on the bed. He would cause his victim's private parts to stop functioning. He would infect his enemy's ankles with foul-smelling ulcers and sores. He would infect his enemy's calves with stinking ulcers and make his thighs rot with pus. These were the vindictive thoughts that occupied Abang Dolah's mind. "He doesn't know who I am! He doesn't know me yet! Bloody fool! I will teach you! I will teach you! Bloody fool!"

Abang Dolah now cast his gaze at Kak Habsah's voluptuous body. Usually, when he looked at her feminine curves, he would feel excited, but that night, he was not aroused at all. At that moment, her body was like a banana stem or a chunk of beef at the market. She gazed at him with desire. Her eyes reflected her hope that she would be satisfied. But he did not react as he usually did. He thought of how he had seized her from her husband. How he used his expertise in winning her over. How the voluptuous woman had surrendered to him voluntarily. He reflected on how she was willing to live in poverty by his side, how she was willing to go hungry.

Then he remembered the secretary's insulting words again. Eleven party members had heard his scorn and insult. Twenty-two pairs of ears and eyes had witnessed the humiliation. "I'll teach you, I'll teach you a good lesson! I will make your stomach bloat. I will make your ankles sore!" whispered Abang Dolah to himself. "As poor as I am, I don't feed off your father's assets! It's not your wife I'm keeping!"

He thought about how the colonisers had succeeded in dividing the Malays with opium, money and women. They had also succeeded in creating chaos by bringing in many immigrants from China and India because the Malays had refused to work in the white men's mines and palm plantations. Abang Dolah was stunned that they had let their own lands be ruled by others, that Malay leaders had learnt to speak English, worn neckties, and gone to London to further their studies. Thinking of these things, he felt happy and proud of those who killed Birch at Pasir Salak. Abang Dolah was proud of warriors like Datok

Bahaman and Mat Kilau. He was proud of Soekarno. They were firm and brave. Being imprisoned had not made Soekarno timid and gutless. Tapered bamboos had taught the Dutch men a lesson; gallons of their blood had been spilled. Thinking of it all, Abang Dolah felt let down by the Malays. Here, many had become the agents of the white men. Far too many were afraid.

WORMS ON TOP OF ONE ANOTHER

THAT EVENING, DURING low tide on the river, Adi spotted several animal carcasses along Lorong 17, their stomachs open and heads already decomposing. It would not be hard for him to find three or four worms for Abang Dolah, who had promised him fifty cents this time for getting him the worms. With a long stick in his hand, Adi raked over a dead rat that he had found. He covered his mouth and nose with a handkerchief. Most of its fur was gone; only a few tufts remained, in spots. The rat's stomach was bloated. Adi poked it with the stick in his hand. The rat's stomach burst with a soft plop. Several white worms sprang out, crawling on top of one another. Adi placed them inside a matchbox and quickly walked back towards Abang Dolah's house.

As promised, Adi received his fifty cents. He then dropped by Bongkok's shop to buy plain biscuits and sugar. Since his father's death, Adi had been feeling lonely. He no longer heard the sounds of his father coughing or quarrelling with his mother. He no longer saw his father praying. Mak Timah now provided for the family by washing clothes for people. When her meagre income of one hundred and twenty dollars a month was used up, she would run out of money for daily expenses. She had yet to pay the fifteen dollars due as house rent. Adi's sister, Ani, had repeatedly invited Mak Timah to live with her. Mak Timah declined; she felt more comfortable living on her own with Adi and Pungut. Ani's rented room was not very big. Pungut often made a big mess and she would defecate all over the place. Moreover, Ani's husband was not that friendly with Mak Timah. Given these problems, Mak Timah felt reluctant to go live with Ani. As a result, Mak Timah would always reply: "Not at the moment, it's not the right time."

Since Pak Mat had died, Adi had taken up a new job. On Friday nights and Saturday nights, he would wash cars at a petrol kiosk at Lorong 18. He would be paid fifty cents for each car. Some nights, Adi managed to wash two to three cars.

There were many prostitutes nearby at Lorong 16. The houses there were decorated with red bulbs. People called this place the red light district. Adi saw many hookers as he washed cars: Malays, Chinese, Indians and even Eurasians. They were pretty and voluptuous. Adi's fellow workmates, who were mostly older than him, often talked about women, about their bodies and their private parts. They would discuss which races of women were good, what kind of women were tempting, and so on.

During the day, if he had free time, Adi would scrounge for aluminium, although these days Dolah

Supik seldom accompanied him. Dolah Supik had gotten a construction job and was at work almost every day. Adi would roam around alone after coming home from school, going to his usual haunts in Kallang Puding and Alkaff Garden. Making fifty cents to one dollar in a day was not that difficult. He would also earn another two to three dollars from washing cars on Friday and Saturday nights. Adi would give the money he earned to Mak Timah. With their combined income, it became possible to pay the monthly house rent and also to buy food for the three of them. Bibik still provided thirty dollars per month for Pungut's milk. As a result, Mak Timah occasionally managed to buy selar kuning fish or small mackerel. Once in a while, she would also buy some vegetables from the market at Lorong 25. Every day there would be rice or porridge to eat—mostly with fried eggs, or to be mixed with soy sauce and fried anchovies. But there would be something to eat every day. Even if there was no rice, there still would be pancakes or biscuits. And so, Adi and his family managed to survive. Adi's sister, Ani, visited them every so often, and would give Mak Timah a dollar or two. Sometimes, Kak Habsah would also give Mak Timah some money. Receiving small amounts of money between Kak Habsah and Mak Timah had become commonplace.

• • •

The General Elections were over. The flame logo party won in many places. The goat's head logo party won in three places. The buffalo's head logo party did not win even a single seat. Adi heard all this information from Abang Dolah.

The police interrogated the stout student who had organised the strike at Geylang-Geylang School. The situation at the school had become calm now.

That evening, Adi was relaxing on the ambin in front of his house. The electrical wires of the street lamp next to the coconut-husk peeler's house had sagged. A torn kite, of which only the bamboo frame remained, was stuck in the wires. The short bamboo pole that had been planted under the banyan tree by the loktang's assistant was missing. The trunk of the banyan tree bore more incision marks than before. Its latex had dried up like scabs and turned blackish. Several joss sticks offered by some Chinese worshippers lay scattered by the roots of the tree. An apple lay rotting. A bowl of rice was half-filled with rainwater. A strong wind was blowing, making the leaves of tree dance. Several whistling thrushes flew to perch on the branches of the banyan tree. The long hanging roots that skimmed the ground still seemed to be wet.

Suddenly, Adi heard a scream from Tong Samboo's house, and then saw her daughter running out. Tong Samboo was right behind her. The girl ran towards the well behind their house. Adi immediately got to his feet to run after her as well. Busuk's husband went after her too, as did the coconut-husk peeler's daughter. Tong Samboo was crying out for help. Her daughter had reached the well, and was raising her leg to place it on the brick wall, in preparation to jump in. Tong Samboo managed to grab hold of her. The girl was struggling and kicking.

"She wants to commit suicide! She wants to commit suicide!" Busuk's husband said.

Tong Samboo then dragged her daughter home by the hair, like someone pulling a cow to its pen. She kept muttering all the while in a language Adi did not understand. Her daughter was screaming as the muscular Tong Samboo pulled her back into their house and slammed the door shut.

Adi thought to himself: Someday, this daughter of Tong Samboo's is going to die. If not by jumping into the well, she will hang herself at the banyan tree, or drink Clorox bleach again. She might cut her wrists with a razor blade. It would be safer if she was sent to the mental hospital.

After that day, Tong Samboo's daughter was tightly guarded. She was not allowed to go out of the house. Adi had not seen Tong Samboo's son, the one who had reportedly violated his sister, since the day he had been taken away. Adi had no idea where the boy had been sent. These days, Tong Samboo did not like to talk to her neighbours. She no longer sat in front of the coconut-husk peeler's house, chatting until nightfall like she used to. In the past, she would occasionally drop by Adi's house to chat with Mak Timah in her bazaar Malay. But now, Tong Samboo no longer wished to mingle with others.

• • •

The days passed by without incident, but then Adi heard from his principal that a major change was in the air. Students who passed the Primary Six examinations this year would be eligible to attend a Malay secondary school. The first Malay secondary school would be opened the next year. Adi was very happy. He also heard that a Malay man had been appointed to the highest office in the country and that thousands of people were busy working together to clean up the city. Abang Dolah told him the salaries of the civil servants had been cut. Adi took in all the news with rapt attention.

Adi continued to wash cars on Friday and Saturday nights. He gained more knowledge from the older boys about prostitutes, what types of cars were expensive and what models were cheap, and also how to siphon off fuel from people's cars and sell it back to them. Once in a while, he would still scrounge for aluminium, and sometimes steal things when there was an opportunity. His sister, Ani, had not visited them for quite some time. She was perhaps disappointed or hurt that Mak Timah had refused to live with her.

Mak Timah had been looking after Pungut all the while. It was now very clear that something was not right with his adopted sister. When her name was called, she would not respond. She showed no reaction and seemed to ignore it. Mak Timah eventually discovered that Pungut was deaf and dumb. On top of all that, her body remained small and she did not grow they way other children did. Pungut did not know how to sit down. She did not know how to crawl. All she could do was remain lying down. The Chinese medium's prediction had apparently come true. Mak Timah was very sad, but she faithfully continued to take care of Pungut. She patiently looked after her, fed her meals and cleaned up her waste. Mak Timah prayed incessantly that Allah would have mercy on Pungut. She prayed that the girl would grow up to be like other children. She said these prayers day and night.

• • •

The roof of Adi's house had been leaking even more than before. The walls were decaying and cracking. The water in the well behind the house was drying up. The only thing going for Adi was that he now had a handy pushcart, kindly made for him by his neighbour Daud Cina using bicycle tyres; he no longer needed to carry water so many times from the communal tap. His pushcart could accommodate six kerosene tins at one go. If the communal tap near his house was crowded, he could fill water from the communal tap opposite Bopeng's shop. It was a little further away, but Adi would not feel so tired. He was the only person who had a pushcart. Adi would never forget Daud Cina's kindness as long as he lived, so much easier was it now for him to fetch water. Usually, he would do so at night, at around eleven or twelve o'clock, when nobody else was carrying water or bathing. One trip would suffice to fill up the jar of drinking water.

To show his gratitude, Adi was willing to pick lottery numbers at a Chinese cemetery in Lorong 3. Adi would draw the numbers, sitting next to a Chinese tombstone. Despite that, Daud Cina never won a draw. He then asked Adi to pick numbers for him at the Bidadari Cemetery, but Adi was afraid to do it there. Daud Cina had once asked Adi to pick numbers under the dead body of a boy who had been killed as he landed on a metal fence. Pak Yahya's son, who fell off a rose apple tree, had landed on a rusty pole that used to be a part of a fence. He died on the spot. The fire brigade arrived to help remove the corpse. Daud Cina had been confident that he would win first prize with the numbers Adi had picked for him, under the boy's corpse. But when Daud Cina bet on the numbers, he did not win anything. A Chinese fishmonger who had picked his numbers along with Adi had won first prize. He became a rich man, so much so that he constructed a beautiful marble grave monument for Pak Yahya's deceased son.

• • •

The leaves of the banyan tree fluttered in the wind, waving at Adi. The hanging roots of the banyan tree swayed. Several starlings and yellow-beaked mynahs flew off the tree at the same time. A mynah perched on Bibik's guava tree. The others flew far away, disappearing out of sight. Adi entered his house to see Mak Timah feeding Pungut porridge.

"Open your mouth, open! Open it!" Mak Timah chided. Adi took the cover off the rice pot. He took a bowl of porridge, poured soy sauce into it and added some anchovies. Then he ate ravenously, even taking a second helping.

"When are you going to your father's grave?" asked Mak Timah.

"Anytime can, Ma."

"Has the cananga plant grown?"

"Yes, but it hasn't bloomed."

"Change it to jasmine."

"Jasmine?"

"Jasmine is suitable for planting on graves," said Mak Timah as she continued to feed Pungut. "When will you have your exams?"

"In three months' time. Still a long way to go."

"Have you paid for your school fees?"

"Yes."

"Will the secondary school cost you lots of money?"

"A lot, a lot, Ma!" Adi suddenly wondered who would pay for his studies if he were to go to secondary school. Adi's grim face made Mak Timah take pity on him.

"Don't worry. As long as I'm still strong, I'll earn some money by washing clothes for as many people as possible. For three or four homes, if necessary," Mak Timah assured him. "As long as I'm still alive and strong!"

MALAYSIA, MALAYSIA

ADI ENTERED THE school hall with some trepidation. Cikgu Majid, the fierce maths teacher who had often slapped Adi, announced the PSLE results. The Primary Six students remained very quiet. Cikgu Majid read out the names of those who had failed in a loud voice, one by one. Adi listened to him nervously. Cikgu Majid looked at the faces of the students before him with piercing eyes. He would pause a bit before reading out the next name, going slowly, deliberately, as if trying to make his students feel more anxious.

"These are the only students who have failed," he finally declared upon finishing the list, looking up at the students before him. Adi's name had not been called. "Those who have failed will have to sit for the exam again next year. Those who have passed will be admitted to secondary school. Now, you may go home!"

The students left the hall, talking loudly among themselves. An overjoyed Adi hummed a tune under his breath. He had passed his examinations and would enter secondary school the next year. He hurried home to inform his mother.

"I passed, Ma, I passed!" Adi cried out, excited.

"Will it cost a lot to study in secondary school?" asked Mak Timah, once again.

This time, Adi said, "I don't know exactly how much it costs yet."

That night, when Abang Dolah came over, Adi told him that he had passed. Abang Dolah shook his hand and congratulated him.

"Well done! Well done! Study hard and take your studies seriously when you enter secondary school," said Abang Dolah. "Let's have a celebration tonight. Come with me to the Padang to watch *Malaysia Night*."

Adi, Kak Habsah, and Abang Dolah took a bus to the Padang. On arriving there, they found that the place was already swarming with thousands of people. The stairs of the City Hall building were decorated with the words *MALAM MALAYSIA* in capital letters.

"Do you know what Malaysia means?" Abang Dolah asked Adi. Adi shook his head.

"Malaysia means Malaya, Sabah, Sarawak and Singapore would be combined to form a federation," explained Abang Dolah. Adi nodded to indicate that he understood.

It was a wonderful night at the Padang. The stars twinkled in the sky and the breeze was cool and refreshing. Abang Dolah, Kak Habsah and Adi tried to inch their way through to the middle of the crowd so that they could get a better look. The festive air made them forget all about the state of turmoil in the country, with some people opposed to the proposed creation of Malaysia. Yesterday some students had gone on a rampage, vandalising government property in secluded areas. Community Centres had become their main targets and they had left scribbled messages on the notice boards. The police had then taken action against them, leading to yet another incident of pursuit and arrest.

"Do you know, Malaysia means a lot to our people?" Abang Dolah said. Kak Habsah did not respond, and instead kept staring at the stage that had been set up on the stairs of City Hall. "Do you know that Malaysia is important for us?" Abang Dolah repeated.

"Why?" asked Adi.

"Because we'll be united again!"

Adi remained silent, waiting for Abang Dolah to go on. Kak Habsah was now munching on fried peanuts. Adi chewed on a cracker. More and more people were flooding into the Padang, even as the night became more beautiful.

"Do you know, I'd never dreamt that we would be united again, never dreamt of it!" Abang Dolah said with a broad smile. "For so long, the colonisers have divided us, cutting off our blood ties! From the early days, we've been separated from the Malay Peninsula—ever since Penang was taken over by the British. Why, ever since Raffles arrived, he wanted to cut us off from the Malay Peninsula."

Kak Habsah kept munching her fried peanuts voraciously, her attention on the musical performance that had started on the stage. Abang Dolah lit up one of his Poker cigarettes. Rings of smoke from his cigarette floated out into the beautiful night. He drew in the smoke repeatedly and then let it out in a strong puff. Rings of smoke moved towards Adi's head.

"But unfortunately, Malaysia means we will merge only with the Malay Peninsula, Sabah and Sarawak. It would be perfect if it included Indonesia as well!" Abang Dolah added, taking another puff of his cigarette. "Do you know, your future's bright! Malay will become the main language in Malaysia! You better study hard when you get into secondary school later."

• • •

For the next few weeks, at coffee shops, by the roadside, in schools, and at home, everyone from politicians to trishaw pedallers was talking about Malaysia. Housewives discussed over their shopping at the markets. The students of Kota-Kota School also talked about it. The radio went on about Malaysia endlessly. Some praised Malaysia, some criticised it. Some were happy with the idea, some disliked it. Even though much else happened, the main topic of discussion remained Malaysia.

The splinter party that had broken away from the axe logo party condemned Malaysia incessantly. More and more demonstrations were held. Arrests became a common sight, as did the incidents of people chasing and beating one another up. That which Adi had never heard of before was now a topic of discussion. People spoke of Malay as the national language. Politicians from the axe logo party talked of the need for everyone to learn the national language. All civil servants, they said, must pass Malay Language examinations. Malay suddenly became more important and esteemed than before. Adi felt proud. Previously, people used to look down on Malay schools and spoke badly of Malay-medium students; now Malay schools were highly regarded.

Students of these schools became very proud; indeed Adi and his schoolmates felt as if in a dream. Adi had never expected such a change. He suddenly felt lucky to have attended a Malay school. He wanted to thank his father for sending him to a Malay school. Malay had become a must if one wanted to get a job in the new Malaysia. Adi felt that his status had risen all of a sudden, and it made him respect the idea of a united Malaysia all the more. He hoped it would materialise soon.

There were increasing rumours that Indonesia did not like the idea of a united Malaysia. Some of Adi's friends from Primary Seven said that Indonesia was going to attack. Meanwhile, within Singapore, those who opposed Malaysia had become bolder. Chinese script graffiti was found scrawled in many places. The community centre at Jurong was vandalised, as was the one at Chua Chu Kang. The Ministry of Education's notice boards had been smeared with paint. While those who liked the idea of a united Malaysia were celebrating, those who opposed it were clearly angry.

In the midst of all this, Adi waited for the new school year, and looked forward to the day he would enter secondary school. He was happy, all the more so since his Malay school had now gained new respect.

Abang Dolah said that there was going to be a referendum. The government planned to find out how many people were in favour of joining Malaysia and how many were against the idea. Only if the majority were in favour would Malaysia be formed. Otherwise, the idea would be abandoned. Adi was quite disturbed to hear that the proposal to join Malaysia might possibly be rejected. If that happened, he thought, Malay would become less important and Malay schools would lose their newfound acceptance.

"Those who are against Malaysia are foolish," Abang Dolah continued, as he sipped at the hot coffee Mak Timah had made for him one evening. "They're foolish! Our country is small. It has no natural resources. If the Communists take control, only then will these people understand! We need to join Malaysia if we are to survive. These people are fools! They've been instigated by the Communists!"

Adi felt a little afraid when he heard Abang Dolah talk of Communists taking control of things. Abang Dolah went on: "They think this country is so big, that it has lots of natural resources. We have no minerals, no rubber, no fish, nothing. Only if the Communists take over, only then will these people realise! They'll be hungry again, like they were under Japanese rule. They'll have to eat tapiocas and wear tattered clothes." He grunted loudly, then sipped his coffee and lit one of his customary Poker cigarettes. He took a deep puff and blew out rings of smoke.

Mak Timah, Adi and Kak Habsah passively listened to Abang Dolah's rant. In the silence that followed, Pungut's mosquito-like voice could be clearly heard from inside the room. The kerosene lamp cast a gloomy light.

Adi went to the window. He stared at the banyan tree. Earlier that evening, he had climbed up the tree carrying a nail with him. Upon reaching the top, he carved the word MALAYSIA onto a branch. The tree's sap had oozed out when he'd etched the name into the bark.

When Bibik came over that night, she also talked about Malaysia. She would have no problems, she said, as she could speak Malay, but people who could not, like Tong Samboo, would be in a difficult position, as would the coconut-husk peeler. Tong San would be the worst off, as he could not speak a single word of Malay.

Abang Dolah reminded Bibik too to vote for Malaysia during the referendum. Pungut's mosquito-like sounds became louder. When Bibik glanced at Pungut, she was shaking her head vigorously. Bibik looked down, sad. She touched her granddaughter's fingers, caressed her scant hair, and gazed long at her face. Pungut continued to shake her head like a loktang and took no notice whatsoever of

Bibik. A downcast Bibik continued to play with the girl's fingers. An oblivious Abang Dolah continued to go on about Malaysia. He complained about the meanness of those who opposed Malaysia and the wickedness of the Communists. His complaints ran late into the night.

Adi wondered how he could earn some more money to buy books, shoes and his new school uniform, and found himself thinking that if his father had been alive, he would have ended up borrowing money from the chetties to buy all of the new school things. Adi knew his father would certainly have been happy to see him go to secondary school. Suddenly, the face of the chetty who asked him to settle his father's loan when Pak Mat had passed away appeared in his mind. The chetty still had not come to claim his money. Perhaps he had forgotten about it, Adi hoped.

UNDER THE KAABAH'S SHELTER

MAK TIMAH WALKED behind Adi, who was holding a bottle of water and several sticks of incense. The two were on their way to visit Pak Mat's grave at Bidadari Cemetery. The atmosphere at the cemetery that evening was serene. The shrill chirping of crickets filled the air. When they reached Pak Mat's grave, Mak Timah told Adi to pour some water on the soil of his father's grave. The cananga plant that Adi had planted was still yet to bloom. Mak Timah squatted by the grave and scattered the jasmine that she had bought from the Lorong 25 market that morning, saying prayers all the while. She then asked Adi to read the Fatihah many times. Adi stared at his father's grave, feeling sad. He wondered how his father was doing, lying in the ground, and if his flesh and bones had already decomposed.

Mak Timah was tearful. Her mind ran over the past and her life with Pak Mat. She thought of her wrongdoings towards him, of his past behaviour, his daily gambling, before he had begun praying regularly at the Kampung Pak Buyung surau. Bibi's dark face appeared in Mak Timah's mind. She recalled how Pak Mat had behaved after he had been afflicted with diabetes. How he had asked for certain special food. How he had asked her to massage his legs and calves. How he had moaned and groaned when pain attacked his bones night after night. Mak Timah began to cry, inconsolable.

The sound of crickets was getting louder. Several graves around Pak Mat's grave had been built up into tombs. They looked clean and neat. Others had not been visited for a long time and were covered with wild grass. Some graves were level with the ground, while the headstones of others were now hidden by tall grasses. Mak Timah sadly wondered who would take care of her grave once she had passed away. If Adi forgot about her after she died, her grave would be covered with weeds and tall grass like the grave next to Pak Mat's.

Mak Timah intended to construct a tomb over Pak Mat's grave, when she had the money. She planned to make it out of durable chengal wood.

She suddenly thought of Ani. Yesterday, her daughter had come over to persuade her to live with her yet again. Mak Timah was still hesitant. She was not used to living with others, and moreover, she did not know Ani's husband very well. Ani's husband was a man of few words; he had a stern look and seldom smiled. Mak Timah still preferred to live with Adi and Pungut until she died or until Adi had grown up and had found himself a job. She did not wish to trouble Ani or to live with an unfriendly son-in-law.

As Mak Timah was about to leave the cemetery, she cried again. She placed her hands on the headstone of Pak

Mat's grave and kept them there for quite a long time. Adi kissed the headstone before leaving, and whispered, "I am about to enter secondary school. I have passed my exams, Father!"

With heavy feet and to the sound of crickets, Mak Timah and Adi left Pak Mat's grave. She turned, now and then, to look back at it. She was still crying.

• • •

Adi's first day at secondary school felt like a dream. The male students of his school had to wear white shirts and trousers, while the female students were required to wear a white baju kurung with a matching blood red sarong. His school was located near the Bidadari Cemetery. Adi was not sure why that particular location had been chosen for the school, although it did allow him to visit his father's grave more frequently. Admittedly, the area was very quiet.

Adi began to learn new subjects. Malay Language was taught almost daily, as was literature. His literature textbook was a novel entitled *Di Bawah Lindungan Kaabah—Under the Kaabah's Shelter—*by the Indonesian author Hamka. He studied science as well. The impressive science laboratory was located next to the main school building. Adi also had to study Religion, History and Geography, along with daily English lessons. It really was a whole new experience.

"All of you are lucky to be able to study in this secondary

school," said Cikgu Bakar, Adi's form teacher, a kind man who smiled a lot. "You are already making history. You must uphold the good name of your school. You are role models and the hope of the nation, who will prove that the Malay secondary school system is a foundation to enter university."

The food at the secondary school canteen was quite expensive; there was nothing available for five cents. Everything on offer cost at least ten cents. A plate of fried noodles cost twenty cents. Half a curry puff cost ten cents. A bowl of bean porridge cost twenty cents. A cup of tea with milk cost ten cents.

This was also the first time Adi had attended a co-ed school, and there were many female students. Bit by bit, Adi was able to buy himself the exercise books that he needed. Straight away, he had purchased *Di Bawah Lindungan Kaabah*, and planned to buy the rest of the textbooks once he had the money. In the meantime, his friend Salleh shared his books with Adi.

Salleh lived on Lorong 21. His father was a gardener. Salleh was very generous and often treated Adi to bean porridge. He was quite tall and had narrow eyes. He even took the time to teach Adi how to draw.

As the days passed, the calls within Singapore for the establishment of Malaysia became louder. A referendum was carried out. The results showed that the majority of people wanted a unified Malaysia, and so, at long last, Singapore merged with the Federation of Malaya, along with Sabah and Sarawak. From then on, Singapore would be part of Malaysia. Breakaway dissidents, formerly of the axe logo party, were still demonstrating by vandalising government property, but Adi was happy at the thought of the newly-formed Malaysia. He once again carved the word MALAYSIA on the banyan tree.

These days, Mak Timah was always short of money. Sometimes Kak Habsah would lend her some. At times Adi's meals consisted only of plain biscuits, in contrast to his usual meal of rice porridge and anchovies mixed with soy sauce. Salleh remained steadfast in helping Adi. He often treated Adi to curry puffs, or divided his own curry puffs in two and gave one half to Adi.

• • •

Adi continued to wash cars on Friday and Saturday nights at the petrol station on Lorong 18. He now also had a new job, assisting Nordin Pendek from the far side of Kampung Pak Buyung to cut down coconut trees on Sundays. Adi helped clean the coconut fronds and received three dollars for his efforts. Sometimes Nordin Pendek was generous enough to give him up to five dollars. As for Mak Timah, in addition to washing people's clothes, she offered massage services to women who had recently given birth, until past their confinement period. Ani still came over and tried to persuade Mak Timah to live with her. Mak Timah continued to reject Ani's invitation.

"It's all right. We might not be affluent. But at least we are independent and we don't trouble others," said Mak Timah.

Abang Dolah continued to visit Adi's house. And he continued to talk about Malaysia.

"How lucky for you Adi, to live in the Malaysian era," Abang Dolah began one night, puffing on his cigarette. "Your future will be bright. You can study with Malay as the medium of instruction right up to the university level."

"There wasn't any Malay university before this?" asked Adi.

"No. There was only Universiti Malaya in Kuala Lumpur, with English as its medium of instruction," explained Abang Dolah. He then saw Adi with *Di Bawah Lindungan Kaabah* and said, "What are you reading? Oh, Hamka's novel. He's a great Indonesian philosopher and religious scholar."

"But I thought that Indonesia doesn't like Malaysia, Abang Dolah."

"Oh, that won't be for long. We're siblings. Don't worry, we will all be united someday. Blood is thicker than water, Adi!"

The leak in the roof of Adi's house was getting even worse. The landlord still refused to replace the roof with a new one. Whenever it rained, the inside of the whole house would get wet. The main pillar was being eaten away by termites and the walls were cracking.

"Next week, you go buy ten to twenty attaps from

Lorong 27 to replace the leaking ones!" Mak Timah told Adi. He absently nodded, engrossed in reading *Di Bawah Lindungan Kaabah*.

• • •

Kak Habsah had finally received a letter of divorce from her husband. Now, after all these years of living with Abang Dolah, she could marry him. Abang Dolah planned to hold a small feast to celebrate.

The leaves of the banyan tree had mostly turned yellow and started to fall. After this season, the tree would begin to bear fruit, which would be tiny and yellowish. Hordes of starlings would gather on and around the banyan tree when this happened. Adi would pick up fallen fruits and penetrate them with the joss sticks used by the Chinese worshippers to make play houses. Ever since Opium-Smoker Uncle had hanged himself from the banyan tree, nobody dared walk under it at night, especially during the full moon; Adi nowadays seldom climbed the tree. He had little free time now. He had to go to school, cut down coconut trees with Nordin Pendek, and wash cars. He had no time even to look for aluminium scrap and rarely did so anymore.

Amid all this commotion, Adi continued with his routine. Salleh continued to help Adi with his drawing. Adi dropped by his father's grave whenever he returned from school. Mak Timah was busy washing people's clothes and giving massages to women who had recently given birth. Abang Dolah's visits to Adi's house, however, became more seldom. His wedding with Kak Habsah was the next week; the feast, it had been decided, would be held at Adi's house since Abang Dolah's room was too small for such an event. Kak Habsah looked forward to her wedding day, all the more since it would come at the end of such a long period of living together with Abang Dolah.

Adi had repaired the leaking roof of his house. He intently studied *Di Bawah Lindungan Kaabah*, and took his English lessons seriously. He and his classmates found their English teacher, Miss Linda, stunningly pretty. Whenever Miss Linda entered the classroom, all the male students in his class would smile, and when she asked them to sit in front on the floor, they would rush to sit near her. Miss Linda would sit on her chair with her legs crossed at the knee. Whenever she moved, all eyes would immediately focus on her legs. English Language was undoubtedly the most popular class among Adi's fellow students.

THE SPECIAL BRANCH

ABANG DOLAH AND Kak Habsah were to be married in four days' time. The wedding had been fixed for Friday, after nightfall.

"We can ask Kak Timah to just make bean porridge!" Kak Habsah proposed, as the couple made their preparations.

"Hey! Don't be so stingy; we can ask her to cook meat curry. We'll serve it with French loaves," Abang Dolah suggested.

"Who do you plan to invite?" Kak Habsah asked, as she straightened the sarong that partially covered her bosom.

"Mail Sengau, Daud Cina, Yusoff, Mama Sulaiman, the imam of the Kampung Pak Buyung surau, and two or three others. Roughly around ten people." His eyes were fixed on Kak Habsah's sarong-clad body, the garment tied just above her breasts. Sometimes Abang Dolah found it strange that they had lived together for so long as man and wife without getting married. Then again, Kak Habsah had never really been comfortable with the arrangement.

"Who's the qadi you've engaged?" Kak Habsah asked as she lay down on the bed.

Abang Dolah stretched out next to her. "Ustaz Idris, my old friend. He knows us. It's easier and he isn't fussy."

"I didn't expect that we'd actually get married," said Kak Habsah softly, as if speaking to herself.

Abang Dolah turned to lie on his side and looked directly into Kak Habsah's eyes. "We are a good match. How we live, how we die, who we marry...these things aren't for us to decide. They're all arranged by Allah!"

"But what will the residents of Kampung Pak Buyung say when they hear that we're going to get married?"

"Why must you care what people say? They'd find fault even if we did something good, let alone if we did something bad. Don't bother about what others might say. All that matters is whether we do what's right for us."

Kak Habsah did not respond. Instead, she stared at the rubber-mat-and-rust-zinc-patched roof. A Chinese song from Ah Kong's Rediffusion next door made her feel sadder still. Tong San's children were shouting and yelling, their voices mingling with the sound of their father loudly clearing his throat.

Next to her, Abang Dolah lay thinking of his first wife, the woman who had given him a son. Images of her face flitted across his mind. She had always been well-dressed and tanned, with a gold-inlaid tooth. He wondered whether she had remarried. A woman accustomed to wealth, she had tended to look down on him, and had wanted all kinds of material things from him: rings, bracelets, necklaces. At that time, Abang Dolah had been a clerk at City Hall, and in no financial position to fulfil his wife's demands.

Still, Allah had blessed him with a son, Zaini. Abang

Dolah realised that he had not seen his son in a long time.

"Just bread and curry?" said Kak Habsah, ending his reverie.

"Yes, that should do. What else do you want besides French loaves and meat curry?"

That night Kak Habsah and Abang Dolah slept soundly. It was cold outside, and dew had started to form on the roof of their house, but inside, the room was bright and filled with anticipation. Kak Habsah had decorated for their wedding night. The floral wallpaper had been changed. Cobwebs had been cleared and the holes in the walls had been plastered up. A new kerosene lamp had replaced the grimy and cracked one. A shelf had been fitted under the mirror on the wall. On it were now laid out Chinese powder, Brylcreem, a comb, and lipstick. Kak Habsah had tidied everything up. She and Abang Dolah now slept with a smile, holding each other in their sleep as though they were already a newlywed couple.

At around two in the morning there was a loud and incessant knocking at their door.

A dazed Abang Dolah woke up, rubbing his eyes. He opened the door to find three men standing there. One of them was stocky, with a short crew cut. The second was an Indian Peranakan. The third man was short and wore a batik shirt.

"Are you Abdullah bin Musa?" the stocky man asked.

"Yes," Abang Dolah replied. He was still in a daze, and was looking about for his spectacles.

"We're from the Special Branch." The stocky man showed his warrant card. "You need to come down to the police station with us, right now."

Abang Dolah was stunned. His heart began to race, blood surged to his head, and his stomach churned.

"Come on! Quick!"

Abang Dolah put on a shirt and trousers and took one last look at Kak Habsah, who had also awakened. Tears welled up in her petrified eyes. She bit her lips to keep from crying.

"Move!"

The man in the batik shirt handcuffed Abang Dolah. Outside, a police car was waiting. Abang Dolah turned around to look at the door of his house. Kak Habsah had started to sob.

Only when the police car began to move off did she burst into tears. Springing to her feet, she rushed to Adi's house. The moment Mak Timah opened the door to let her in, Kak Habsah threw her arms around the other woman.

"Abang Dolah's been arrested! Abang Dolah's been arrested!" Kak Habsah managed to say, in between wails. The sound of her wailing woke Adi up. He came to her, clearly surprised.

Mak Timah sat her down at the ambin. "Calm down! Calm down!" she urged. "Who arrested Abang Dolah? Why?"

Kak Habsah kept sobbing and did not answer.

"Who arrested him? Why? Why?" Mak Timah repeated.

"Police! The Special Branch police!" Kak Habsah burst out.

"Why?"

A puzzled Adi stared at the tearful Kak Habsah.

"I've no idea, I don't know why," she replied shortly. She began to weep again.

Mak Timah tried to calm her down. "Be patient. Tomorrow we'll go to the police station and find out why Abang Dolah's under arrest. Be patient! We can't do anything now and moreover, it's still dark. Tomorrow, early in the morning, we can go down to the police station. It's all right, don't cry."

Kak Habsah began to speak. "What has Abang Dolah done wrong? He hasn't stolen anything! He hasn't beaten anybody up! Why did the police arrest him? Why? What crime could he be guilty of?"

Mak Timah and Adi did not reply. They could only wonder in silence and fear the worst.

Kak Habsah stayed at Adi's house until morning. Her eyes were swollen from crying all night. As soon as it was light, Mak Timah and Kak Habsah sought out Mail Sengau to ask him to accompany them to the police station. Kampung Pak Buyung was already astir. News of Abang Dolah's arrest spread quickly. According to Daud Cina, Abang Dolah was not the only person to have been arrested. Hundreds of people had also been placed under arrest at the same time all over the country. He had heard over the radio that most of them were political activists.

Only then did Kak Habsah realise why Abang Dolah had been taken away. She was now certain that it had something to do with his political activities with the goat's head party.

"It's suspected that they're involved with the Communists," explained Daud Cina.

When Kak Habsah, Mak Timah and Daud Cina went to the police station, they were not allowed to meet with Abang Dolah since the police were still conducting their investigation. Kak Habsah started crying again. That evening, some policemen came again to Abang Dolah's house. They rummaged through all of Abang Dolah's books and went through every one of his files. Kak Habsah cursed at the policemen, the ones who had arrested Abang Dolah. She maintained that he was a good, innocent man who was not a Communist. News of Abang Dolah's arrest spread far and wide, like an endless cascade, giving rise to all kinds of speculation and all sorts of predictions. Adi was saddened by Abang Dolah's arrest. He knew that Abang Dolah had never considered himself a Communist. He shared Kak Habsah's loss and sorrow.

• • •

For an entire week, Kak Habsah trudged to and from the Central Police Station. Not once had she been allowed to meet with Abang Dolah. Day after day, she went home dejected. She constantly kept muttering that Abang Dolah was innocent and that he was not a Communist.

"There go my marriage plans, Sister," she said to Mak Timah, even as she began to cry yet again. "Abang Dolah had already gotten himself his baju Melayu. He'd planned to hold a feast. Everything is ruined, Sister. Ruined!"

"Be patient, Habsah. Be patient. Dolah will soon be released. He's not a criminal!"

"We wanted to start life afresh by getting married. Yet, this is what we get! This is how people treat us!" Kak Habsah asked Mak Timah to pray for Abang Dolah's quick release. She said that she would wait patiently for him to return.

The villagers had many theories about Abang Dolah's arrest. Some speculated that he would never be released, that he would be imprisoned for a very long time. Some said that he would be jailed for three years; others said seven. Still others claimed that Abang Dolah had been framed by one of the other political parties. Some even said that what had happened to him was retribution for having practised witchcraft.

Adi was sad to lose Abang Dolah. He had lost the one person to whom he could turn for guidance. He went to Kak Hasbah's house, and she showed him the baju Melayu that Abang Dolah had planned to wear on their wedding day and the songkok that he had bought to go with it. Sobbing all the while, she also showed Adi the baju kurung and the embroidered songket that Abang Dolah had bought for her. Kak Habsah continued to go every day to the police station, and upon coming home, she would complain about the policemen who had arrested him.

The more than a hundred people who had been arrested were all suspected of conspiring to disturb the peace and being involved in Communist activities. The news of their arrests was aired frequently over the radio and splashed across the newspapers. Abang Dolah's arrest remained on everyone's lips in Kampung Pak Buyung. Mak Timah continued to advise Kak Habsah to be patient and to remain calm.

• • •

Adi attended school as always. His workload seemed to increase even further. He had memorised the plot of Hamka's novel *Di Bawah Lindungan Kaabah*; Mak Timah would often ask Adi to read the book out loud in his free time. Of late, Ani came to visit Mak Timah less and less. Adi hardly climbed the banyan tree any longer. Instead, he would simply stare at its branches and leaves from afar. As usual, Chinese worshippers would place fruits and burn incense under the tree. Starlings continued to perch on the branches at dusk. Tong Samboo's daughter would lift her skirt up whenever someone passed by her house. Bibik would drop in frequently to talk about Abang Dolah, who remained in detention. Kak Habsah would linger at Adi's house almost every night, waiting fervently and with solemn prayers, for Abang Dolah to be freed. She waited for her wedding day.

THE WHITE MEN'S DOG

THE ATMOSPHERE AT Adi's school was one of jubilation and excitement. The students set about their studies with enthusiasm. A united Malaysia had given newfound importance to the Malay language and the students of Adi's school could now hold their heads high even in front of students from English schools. The situation now was such that those who could not speak Malay struggled to quickly learn it. In Malaysia, it was expected, everyone would have to pass at least Primary One level examinations in Malay. As a result, thousands of people suddenly wanted to learn Malay.

Adi had heard that Singapore would become the "New York of Malaysia". It was planned that a national mosque would be erected at the Padang as a symbol of Islam and a united Malaysia. Adi was delighted. The grandest mosque ever built. It was all like a dream. He felt very fortunate, and as though he was in the midst of a great carnival. New campaigns and events such as Malay Language Week and Malay Language Month turned out to be fascinating. From trishaw pedallers to ministers, everyone raced to learn the language.

Abang Dolah was jailed without trial and transferred to Changi Prison. Kak Habsah was now allowed to see him once a week. It was hard for Adi to understand what crime Abang Dolah had committed; it was not as if he had committed a murder, or was a robber or a rapist. Kak Habsah, however, was just happy to be able to see Abang Dolah on weekends.

"Abang Dolah is fine. He seems to have put on some weight," Kak Habsah told Mak Timah. "He's allowed to read books and newspapers."

"Did he ask about me?" asked Adi, looking up from the book that he had been reading.

"Yes, he did. He sends a message asking you to study hard," replied Kak Habsah. "What book are you reading?"

"*Panglima Awang* by Harun Aminurrashid. Awang was a strong Malay warrior who fought against the Portuguese," explained Adi. "My school is going to stage a drama based on the book. Please come with my mother to watch it. They have all kinds of shows to coincide with Malay Language Month, Sister. There'll be dramas, dances, quizzes and many such events. Please come!"

"How are your studies? Are they difficult?" asked Kak Habsah. In spite of her despair, she still bothered to find out about Adi's schooling. For his part, Adi regarded Kak Habsah as his own sister. He had heard the residents of Kampung Pak Buyung say many bad things about her— Kak Habsah kept men, Kak Habsah had cheated on her husband, she was a loose woman—all sorts of things. But, Adi felt that Kak Habsah was a good person. She was sincere and helped those in need. It was enough to make him think of her as a sister and he now addressed her as such.

"It's quite difficult, Sister. English is hard. So are Maths and Science. What I hate most, though, is Art. If I draw a table, it will look like a frog," Adi said, laughing. Kak Habsah and Mak Timah both joined in.

"What subject do you like most, Adi?" Kak Habsah asked.

"Malay language and literature. I always score well in these two subjects," said Adi. He then suddenly changed the topic. "When will you be seeing Abang Dolah again? Can I come along?"

Kak Habsah grimaced slightly. Perhaps, she wondered what Abang Dolah was doing in prison at that moment, or she possibly remembered the shawl and the baju kurung suit that Abang Dolah had bought for her. Or perhaps, she imagined her postponed wedding night with Abang Dolah.

"Sure. Come with me this Saturday. He misses you too."

"Can Mother come along too?"

"Of course, if she wants to join us," Kak Habsah replied, pushing back the strands of hair that had fallen on her cheek. Her once chubby face was now thin, and her eyes no longer sparkled. Her batik sarong had faded, as had her frilly kebaya. "All right, all three of us can go. Abang Dolah will be happy to be able to see you and Mak Timah." She then grew quiet as she fell deep into thought.

Kak Habsah gazed out the open window, at the banyan tree. The twisted roots seemed to mimic the turmoil in her mind. She recalled the face of her former husband, Omar. He had been a brawny, short-tempered fellow who had liked to beat her up. But brawn had been Omar's only strength. Kak Habsah had known well about his weaknesses—his masculinity did not match up to his brute strength. He would beat Kak Habsah up when his lust was not satiated, but the fault had not been hers. Omar had been often impotent and even after seven years, Kak Habsah had not become pregnant. Life with Omar had been hell for her; the contrast between Abang Dolah and Omar was stark, like sky and earth. Abang Dolah, despite being poor, was kind-hearted. He was gentle and both able and willing to satisfy Kak Habsah's sexual needs at any time. A simple man, Abang Dolah was not fussy and would eat whatever was served.

Kak Habsah had first met Abang Dolah at a wedding. He had won her admiration with his skilful handling of the violin. The lanky man had seemed to possess an extraordinary artistic appeal. Since that day, she had been unable to forget Abang Dolah's gentle and calm face and his soothing music.

• • •

That night, after Kak Habsah had gone home, Adi sat with his copy of *Panglima Awang*. He looked up from the book every now and then to chat with his mother.

Mak Timah sat sewing a dress for Pungut. One of the

earpieces on her spectacles had broken off and her glasses were held in place over the other ear by the remaining temple arm.

"Why does Abang Dolah refuse to work? He's smart and graduated from an English school," asked Adi.

"I have no idea," replied Mak Timah softly.

"My teacher said that Malays are lazy. We love the arts, music and entertainment, but not work."

Mak Timah cast a sad glance at Adi. She saw Pak Mat's face when she looked at Adi's thick eyebrows. "I don't know. That could be the reason. Perhaps he's lazy," she replied, turning back to her sewing.

"Is Abang Dolah lazy? He only loves music, he plays the violin and refuses to work," asked Adi again. He remembered what his literature teacher had said: *The Malays have historically been laid-back people. They love only entertainment and things related to the arts. They live a contented life. As long as they have some food to eat and something to wear, they are satisfied. Other cultures are different. They work all day and night to gain wealth, and when they end up ruling our country, we get upset. But we don't realise that we are the lazy ones.*

Adi was surprised that Abang Dolah refused to work. He was a spirited man, active in politics. He loved his people and his country and wanted to defend the poor and the oppressed. Yet, he did not want to work. He did not want to use his intelligence to seek money. Adi found the contradictions perplexing.

Adi flipped a page of his novel, thinking of an argument he had recently had with Ali, a Raffles School student who also lived at Kampung Pak Buyung. Adi had tried to defend Abang Dolah, with words similar to the ones Mak Timah had just used.

"Abang Dolah is really a typical Malay. An old breed Malay, a lazy bum!" Ali had said all this in a disparaging way.

"Abang Dolah is not lazy. He just doesn't want to work for the white men," Adi had said. "He says that the white men consider the Malays lazy because they refused to work in the white men's tin mines and their palm and rubber plantations. That's why the white men think Malays are lazy. Abang Dolah purposely refuses to work for the white men. He's not lazy!" He then glared at Ali.

"Did the white men ask Abang Dolah? Did they ask him to work in their mines? Did they? Did they ask him to cut down timber? He's simply lazy!" Ali added with a smirk. He had continued to insult Abang Dolah, before finally asking Adi, "Does Abang Dolah pray? Does he pray?"

"I have no idea," replied Adi.

"Don't tell me you know nothing. You live near him. You learnt to recite the Quran from him. How can you not know?" Ali teased. "People who don't pray are Communists, you know!"

"You may be a Raffles student, but you really are very dense. Are you saying that everyone who prays is a Muslim? Don't the Chinese pray? The white men don't pray like us. But are they Communists?"

"I'm not talking about the Chinese. I'm not talking about the white men. I'm talking about us, the Malays. Muslims must pray! That's the reason why Abang Dolah was accused of conspiring with the Communists, because he doesn't pray! He doesn't, right?"

"I don't know. I don't know," Adi said.

"He keeps somebody's wife, right? Kak Habsah is the wife of another man, right? He's not married to her, is he? That's how Communists live, you know! He's also a bomoh, right? A bomoh who practises witchcraft on others? That's typical of the old Malays. Casting black magic spells on people, destroying their own race. Why didn't Abang Dolah cast a spell on the white men? Why does he do it on his own race? It serves him right that he was arrested! Serves him right!"

Adi's anger had reached its peak. He had spewed expletives at Ali, who had then chased him. "You attend an English school," Adi yelled behind him. "So you want to be the white men's dog! The white men's dog!"

• • •

Abang Dolah's face and his sunken eyes flashed across Adi's mind. He thought of his neighbour's bohemian lifestyle. He was good at reciting from the Quran and he was well-versed in religion, yet Adi had never seen him perform his prayers. He loved his country, but he also despised the white men. He was good at playing the violin and was gentle, compassionate and lived a simple life. He disliked seeing people suffering from poverty. But then, Adi wondered, why did Abang Dolah refuse to work? Why did Adi hardly see him pray? The questions came at Adi one after the other. He had no answers.

Adi tried to imagine what Abang Dolah might be going through, in prison. He would, Adi supposed, feel lonely, and he certainly would miss Kak Habsah. He could no longer smoke his Poker cigarettes, nor could he drink Mak Timah's strong coffee. Kak Habsah had carefully preserved the songkok and baju kurung that Abang Dolah had bought. Adi guessed that Abang Dolah had probably wanted to turn over a new leaf. He had wanted to marry Kak Habsah and make their relationship a legitimate one. And then, he might have found a job to provide for Kak Habsah. Perhaps Kak Habsah could have given up working as a maid. Perhaps Abang Dolah would be a responsible husband. He would likely begin performing his prayers after marrying Kak Habsah.

"Life is transitory, Adi. Nothing is permanent," Abang Dolah had once said. "We must do good deeds. Our lives are meaningless if we live for seventy or eighty years and leave nothing behind when we die. We don't live just to eat or to amass money. A man must do good deeds in his life, Adi. He must do something for the oppressed. Our country is impoverished and undeveloped. We must dare to sacrifice something, anything, to free our nation from its colonial fetters. Remember, Adi, when you have grown up, when you have graduated from secondary school and university, remember the sufferings of your people. Don't become like peas that forget their pod, like all those who went to university, succeeded and then became wealthy and had beautiful wives, only to forget the plight of their own people. They even sided with the colonisers. They became the colonisers' dogs, their agents! Don't you become like that, Adi. If you lived such a life, your life would be no different than that of a dog! Animals live for their stomachs! Remember, Adi! The white men have colonised our minds and souls!"

Adi woke up in the middle of the night, when he heard his mother coughing badly. The sound was loud and heavy. The kerosene lamp on the wall was dim, the kerosene in it nearly finished. Pungut continued to sleep without stirring. Mak Timah then coughed again, a long, wracking cough. Adi got up and went to his mother. She was rubbing her chest. She covered her mouth with a rag spotted in red blotches.

"Ma, are you coughing blood?" His mother looked at him sternly, though she was clearly in pain.

"My chest hurts, Adi. Please get me the medicated oil from the drawer in the kitchen," said Mak Timah.

"Have you taken some cough mixture?" Adi asked as he headed for the kitchen. The kerosene lamp in the kitchen had gone out completely. Adi searched for some matches.

He removed the lamp's chimney and lit the wick again. He then rummaged through the drawer of his old cupboard. Inside this cupboard, his mother kept fish, chilli sauce, rice, vegetables and other dried foods. His fingers touched a bottle of Axe oil. There was very little left in it, but Adi brought it over to his mother anyway. She took the bottle from Adi, poured a few drops on her palm and rubbed it into her chest.

"Have you taken the cough mixture?" asked Adi again.

"There's no more left. You go and buy it for me from the sinseh's shop tomorrow," Mak Timah said, trying to stifle her cough.

"I'll make some tamarind juice for you. It's good for cold. Your chest has heated up. That's why you're coughing up blood." Adi went into the kitchen again. He reached for a basket on top of a cupboard for the tamarind. The dim light of the lamp revealed that only a little of this was left as well. Adi took out a saucer and filled it with water from the earthenware jar. He mixed the tamarind into the water and then poured the mixture into a glass, filling it up about a quarter of the way. It looked muddy and unclear.

"Here it is, Ma. Please have a sip," Adi said. Mak Timah accepted the chipped glass and drank its contents. Adi's remedy proved quite effective—Mak Timah continued to cough, but she no longer brought up blood.

"Please see a doctor tomorrow, Ma. The one at Lorong 25."

"I don't have any money. It will cost at least five dollars."

"I have some money. I have two dollars, which I earned from washing cars yesterday. You can add two or three dollars. That should do." Adi studied his mother's face by the dim light of the kerosene lamp. She looked pale.

"Let me see. If it doesn't get better by tomorrow, I'll go," replied Mak Timah, lying down again.

"You can't wait and see, Ma. You've been coughing up blood. You need to see a doctor tomorrow."

Mak Timah continued to cough through the night, but she did not bring up blood anymore. Nevertheless, every time she coughed, Adi would wake up and check on her.

The next day, when Adi again insisted that his mother see the doctor at Lorong 25, Mak Timah declined. She said, "It's all right. I've stopped coughing. There's no need to see a doctor now." Adi tried to coax his mother into going, but to no avail.

"If you cough again tonight, you must see a doctor tomorrow, you must!"

• • •

At school, Adi's mind was ill at ease. He constantly thought about his mother's health and was worried that she might have been stricken with a chronic cough. The thought of his mother coughing incessantly and bringing up blood disturbed Adi to no end. He could not focus on his literature lesson. To add to his restlessness, he was called to the principal's office, even though he had no idea what he might have done. As far as he knew, his school fees were caught up and settled.

Adi entered the principal's office. He was asked to sit down. Adi bowed respectfully. His fierce-looking principal only made him feel more unsettled.

"You've been awarded the bursary that you'd applied for. The amount is seventy-five dollars per year. Tomorrow, please come with your mother to the office to receive the money"

Relief hit Adi like a wave. He had completely forgotten about the bursary that he had applied for three months before. And the following day, he would receive seventy-five dollars. It was quite a substantial amount. His thoughts turned back to his mother. Adi decided to call a doctor to his house if his mother refused to go see one. With the bursary money, he could pay a home visit fee, which he estimated would be up to ten or fifteen dollars. More money could always be earned; his mother's health was more important.

By the time Adi returned to his classroom, his literature teacher had stepped out, and his mathematics lesson had begun. Adi had no interest in mathematics. His maths teacher was as fast as a train with his explanations. He was also fierce-looking and his voice was rough, often looking down on the students by saying, "Malays are stupid when it comes to mathematics. They are good in music though. They are good in singing too!" His maths teacher would often pass such snide remarks whenever his students could not understand his lessons.

The moment Adi reached home, he looked for his mother. Mak Timah had just finished bathing Pungut and was now feeding her. Pungut had blue ribbons in her hair and she smelled of talcum powder. Pungut often slept late and would stay awake when everyone else was fast asleep at night. Left to herself, she would fiddle with her own fingers, shake her head from side to side and make her usual, mosquito-like sound.

"Are you still coughing, Ma?" asked Adi.

"No. I'm fine now," replied Mak Timah as she fed Pungut.

"I've received a bursary worth seventy-five dollars a year. The principal has requested that you come to school tomorrow to take the money," Adi said. He then asked, impulsively, "Ma, may I buy a bicycle?"

"How much will it cost?"

"A secondhand one won't be expensive. I can get it for thirty or forty dollars," said Adi. Mak Timah nodded her assent.

The next day Mak Timah went to Adi's school to receive the bursary. Three days later, Adi started cycling to school. He had bought a used black bicycle for thirty-five dollars from a shop at Lorong 29. Adi felt like he was in a dream. After years of walking to school, he now had his own bicycle. Lost in rapture, he wheeled freely around

Kampung Pak Buyung. He guarded it as though it were made of gold.

It was now easy for Adi to move about. He could reach the market at Lorong 25 in less than ten minutes and Bopeng's shop in less than five. It took him only twenty minutes from his house to his school. Adi felt weightless as he cycled fast, daydreaming all the while about his future and the job that he might get now that he was more mobile.

• • •

Things soon got very busy at Adi's school, as the students prepared to celebrate National Language Week. The students were busy rehearsing the drama *Panglima Awang*. Some, including Adi, practised reciting poems. Adi was to read Masuri S.N.'s poem "Seribu Harapan"—"A Thousand Hopes". His literature teacher had selected it for him, saying that Adi had a voice well-suited to reading poetry. Adi memorised the poem and repeated it wherever he went, when he was cycling, bathing, taking water from the well, fetching water from the communal tap, and while looking at the banyan tree. Adi didn't actually fully understand the content of the poem, but he felt highly energised when he recited the words. His literature teacher had told him that the poem was about a young man like Adi, who lived in the Malaysia of the future. It held brilliant hope for the future of the Malays and Malay-medium schools and promised many other things.

Adi's mother stopped coughing, and he gradually stopped worrying. At the end of the General Elections, the flame logo party had won in many areas. The axe logo party was defeated badly. Everyone talked about how great the flame logo party was, and how they had won in a clean sweep. Adi did not bother very much with the elections, though he still did think of Abang Dolah and wondered when he would be released. Kak Habsah looked thinner and she was no longer as cheerful as before. She had become aloof, giving curt replies if Mak Timah were to ask her something, and she had no interest in joking around with Adi anymore. Adi often went to Kak Habsah's house to keep her company, and nearly every time she would get out the shawl Abang Dolah had given her, as well as the songket suit and Abang Dolah's songkok and his baju kurung that he had ordered for their wedding. Predictably, she would talk about her postponed wedding and swear anew at the policemen who had arrested her future husband.

• • •

More and more people were actively learning the Malay language. Everyone wanted to speak Bahasa Melayu. Many campaigns were held to encourage people to speak Malay. The proposed grand mosque at the Padang had yet to be built, and the promises to transform Singapore into "Malaysia's New York" were yet to be implemented, but Adi felt hopeful. His lessons in school were getting harder, especially mathematics, science and arts. He was more interested in literature and had borrowed many books from the school library. He was already familiar with Tongkat Warant, Keris Mas, Noor S.I. and Harun Aminurashid. Adi's interest in literature grew deeper still. He did well in the subject during every examination. When Kak Habsah showed him Abang Dolah's book collection, Adi got very excited about the many Indonesian books. He began to learn about Hamka. He developed an interest in Sutan Takdir Alisjabana. He began to love Mokhtar Lubis. Adi truly loved to read now. Sometimes he would climb the banyan tree, sit on one of the topmost branches and read a book, uncaring of the monitor lizard that would now and then come out from among the roots.

Adi still bathed with cold water from the moss-coated well. He would still pluck some hibiscus from next to the well. A Chinese family now lived in Kak Salmah's house, but whenever Adi passed by it, he would remember Kak Salmah drinking samshu and beating Jamilah up.

Mak Timah had a coughing fit every now and then; she would tremble and tears would flow as she fought against the pain in her chest, but she no longer coughed up blood. Once again, Adi became worried about his mother's condition. Mak Timah still refused to see a doctor. Whenever she had one of her bad coughs, Kak Habsah would rub her chest if she were around. Sometimes, Ani would rub her chest instead, when she came to visit. It was the only thing that brought Mak Timah some relief.

RIOTS

ADI RUSHED HOME. He was terrified and his whole body was trembling. Drops of sweat trickled down from his forehead onto his cheeks. He was breathing hard and his heart was pounding. When a worried Mak Timah asked him what had happened, he found himself unable to speak.

"People are fighting! People are fighting!" Adi eventually gasped. "A riot has taken place!"

Mak Timah did not understand what he was saying. "Who? Who's fighting? Who's rioting? Where?" she asked in a single burst.

Adi tried to get ahold of himself. He went into the kitchen, poured himself a glass of tea from a chipped teapot, and drank it down in a single gulp.

"Who? Who? Who's fighting? Adi, who's rioting?"

"The residents of Kampung Pak Buyung are all running for cover. Everyone is staying indoors. No one dares to come out."

"But who's fighting against who? What's going on?"

"Lots of people are fighting and rioting! Many others are running away from Lorong 12," Adi explained.

A short while later Bibik came to their house. She cautioned Mak Timah and Adi not to go anywhere. If there was an emergency, she told them, they were to quickly come to her house. "If Habsah comes to you, tell her to stay indoors. If she's afraid, she can also come to my house," Bibik said, before hurrying back home.

Kak Habsah arrived soon after Bibik left. Her face was pale and she looked nervous. She carried a small transistor radio in her hand.

"We can't go out, Adi. You can't go to school. There's a riot going on! A riot!" Kak Habsah exclaimed. "It's a racial riot, a racial riot! It started from a Maulud Nabi procession. Today is the Prophet Muhammad's birthday, you know. We can't go out. I will have to stay here."

Mak Timah looked worried as she came to understand the situation. Adi, Mak Timah and Kak Habsah sat on the ambin. Kak Habsah brought her transistor radio near to her ear; the battery was running low, and the sound that came from it was distorted and unclear.

"Everyone is advised to remain calm, stay indoors, not to go out on to the streets, and not to carry weapons," relayed the message broadcast over the air. Adi tried to peep out through a slit in the wall. He saw several people running through the kampung; they were carrying metal pipes, parangs, bicycle chains, wooden bars, and bottles in their hands. Adi did not tell his mother what he saw, worried that it would frighten her more. He then sat down next to Kak Habsah again.

"Remain calm. Don't be influenced by rumours." Kak Habsah continued to relay the radio broadcaster's directions. There was a knock at the door. Adi peeped out through the view-hole. It was Bibik. Pungut's father was with her. Adi quickly opened the door.

"Come, stay at my house, come!" Bibik said. "It's not safe here! Come, when everything is safe again, you can return." The situation indeed felt unsafe. Every time Adi peeped out through the hole in the wall he could see several more young men running around with weapons in their hands. Some of the faces seemed familiar to Adi but others were not. They all rushed around, looking fierce.

Adi suddenly wondered what had befallen the other residents of Kampung Pak Buyung. They might have been hacked to death, their houses attacked or burnt down. "Come, don't delay, it's safer at my house; no one will hurt us. Come quick," Bibik insisted.

This time, Mak Timah agreed. She took her shawl, grabbed hold of Pungut, and was ready to leave. Accompanied by Pungut's father, Mak Timah, Kak Habsah, Adi and Pungut quickly walked to Bibik's house.

Kak Habsah held her radio close to her ear all the while. "There's a curfew tomorrow, no one is allowed to go outdoors," she said. Already, they noticed, several policemen were around. The group reached Bibik's house to find Pungut's mother, Busuk, and her other children, Pungut's siblings, also listening to the radio.

They all stayed at Bibik's house until nightfall. Adi thought about his friends. How was Dolah Supik? How was Yunos Potek? And Kassim Boca? Were they all safe? What about the imam of the surau?

Bibik made some Chinese tea. Pungut sat next to Mak Timah, shaking her head in her usual way. It was the first time that Pungut's siblings had met her, even though they had always lived close by.

"This is all because of those damned gangsters! Curse them!" railed Bibik. "For hundreds of years we've been living together, like brothers, without any fights, and now they all want to fight each other! Curse those gangsters!"

Mak Timah remained silent. Kak Habsah was still holding her transistor radio close to her ear. Pungut's siblings stared at their sister as she shook her head and made her usual mosquito-like noise. Pungut's mother, Busuk, had not come out of her room for a while. Pungut's father was in the kitchen. When Adi peeped out through the view hole in the door, he saw several policemen on patrol outside, anti-riot police like the ones he had seen when the students of the Chinese school had gone on the rampage. These policemen were equipped with helmets, shields, and truncheons. Several gas canisters were hung at their waists. If Abang Dolah had been free, he would certainly have been accused of conspiring to cause these riots. Maybe, Adi thought, it was fortunate that Abang Dolah was still in jail.

• • •

That night when Mak Timah wanted to go home, Bibik tried to stop her. But Mak Timah insisted, so Bibik decided to accompany her and spend the night over at their house. Adi, Mak Timah, and Kak Habsah were overwhelmed with fear. Pungut knew nothing.

"Don't be afraid, they know this is a Malay house. They won't disturb us. Don't be afraid, I'm here," Bibik said, trying to raise their spirits. All night long, Mak Timah recited every prayer that came to mind, her lips constantly moving. Kak Habsah and Adi also said some prayers.

In the morning, a curfew was imposed. Bibik went back and forth from Adi's house, constantly checking on him and his family. She did not let Adi go to Bongkok's shop to buy anything. Anything Mak Timah needed, Bibik's son-in-law bought for her. They heard the news over the radio that some people had been killed and many others were injured. Mak Timah became even more anxious. She continued to recite her prayers without pause. Adi felt imprisoned; Mak Timah did not let him go out. In fact, he was not even allowed to show his face at the window. Adi spent his time reading, but his mind often wandered to the other residents of Kampung Pak Buyung. Some, he knew, had fled to their relatives' houses in Geylang Serai. Others had gone to Kampung Melayu.

• • •

The curfew lasted for three days, after which the situation came under control. Things were calm again, and people began to go to work and move about as before. Adi too went back to school. The peace lasted for about two months, after which another riot broke out. Bibik again took the trouble to look after Mak Timah, Kak Habsah and Adi. Things seemed to be even worse this time around. Rather than police, Adi saw soldiers on guard, carrying rifles with bayonets attached. Many soldiers from the Malay Peninsula could be seen on duty as well. Five or six of these soldiers would patrol the most sensitive areas. The news on the radio was that many people were dead and hundreds of others were injured. A curfew was again imposed. Then, as before, the situation returned to normal. People went back to work and to their daily routines.

However, Mak Timah was now afraid to stay any longer at Kampung Pak Buyung. Kak Habsah felt the same way, as did Adi. If another riot occurred, it could prove to be very dangerous for them, and how long could Bibik continue to keep them safe?

That night, Bibik came over yet again to Adi's house. Kak Habsah was helping his mother cook the already-late meal; Mak Timah had come down with another bout of coughing, aggravated by having to wash clothes at Lorong 25 and Lorong 33 before going to Lorong 40 to give a massage to a woman who had recently given birth. Adi was lying down on the ambin with a kerosene lamp before him, captivated by a novel entitled *Salina* by A. Samad

Said. He felt as though the characters in the novel were real, and all the incidents were happening before his very eyes. Bibik considered Adi for a while and then said it was good of him to study so hard. She reminded him not to forget how his poor mother had struggled to raise him, once he was grown up and had started working. Adi met her reminder with a smile. Bibik spent a few minutes with Pungut and then began talking to Mak Timah.

"I think you should just move to Geylang Serai, Timah. It's safer there," Bibik suggested. The idea had indeed already presented itself to Mak Timah, and she had been mulling over it for the past few weeks.

"It's not that I don't like to live near you, Timah; we've become like sisters. But I'm afraid that if there's a riot again, these gangsters will cause serious trouble. If something bad happens, you will have a hard time. I'm afraid that I won't be able to take care of you every time there's a riot."

"I've been thinking the same. Habsah too thinks so," replied Mak Timah, looking sadly at Bibik. The elderly woman was indeed very kind and she also loved her granddaughter Pungut. Being a Peranakan, Bibik truly understood the Malay lifestyle.

"I'll be sad when you move away, and it will be difficult for me to see Pungut. You've been living here for over twenty years, among the Chinese. What to do; it's not that we are fighting with each other, but these damned gangsters won't care if we are old, or have little kids. They would just kill us all."

Mak Timah was indeed afraid to stay there any longer, even though the rent was low. Many of Kampung Pak Buyung's residents had already moved to Geylang Serai, Kampung Ambar, Siglap, Jalan Eunos and other safer areas.

"This Sunday, Habsah and I will look for a house," she announced. Bibik gave Pungut a sad glance, thinking of their inevitable separation.

• • •

That night, Mak Timah and Kak Habsah busily discussed their plan to look for a house to rent. Kak Habsah suggested they consider the Geylang Serai area. Adi felt sad at the thought of being forced to move; although his house was rundown and had a leaky roof, even though he had to carry water from the communal tap or draw water from the well, he loved to live there. He would be separated from his beloved banyan tree. It had been his friend since the days when he could not read. Its roots and branches seemed to hold his smell within them and the monitor lizards now knew him well. Adi would be forced to leave his neighbours behind. He imagined how terrible he would feel when the time came to move away.

HINDI SONGS, TAJ CINEMA

MAK TIMAH AND Kak Habsah managed to rent two barrack houses, side by side, at Jalan Turi in Geylang Serai. The rent was thirty-five dollars per month. The seven units in the barracks shared a drum-bowl type latrine with pipe water. There was an altar to a Chinese deity in the building, and not too far from it stood a mosque. The house was very close to the market, and Adi could reach his school within forty minutes on his bicycle. Lorong 25 and Lorong 33, where Mak Timah went to wash clothes, were also not too far.

Bibik had been the saddest about their departure. She had cried uncontrollably and hugged and kissed Pungut many times. Adi too had felt very sad when the lorry taking them away had begun to move. He'd gazed at the banyan tree for a long time and then had turned to his house with tears in his eyes. Just the previous day, Adi had climbed the tree, the word MALAYSIA still visible on the branch where he had carved it. Adi had felt like hugging the banyan tree, but its trunk was too thick for him to reach around it. As the lorry exited the compound of his house, Adi let a tear fall. Bibik and Pungut's mother accompanied Adi to his new house. They waited until all the belongings had been taken off the lorry and then made to leave. Bibik cried again and hugged and kissed her granddaughter repeatedly. Pungut remained quiet.

This would be Adi's first experience of living solely among Malays. The Geylang Serai area was busy. Hindi songs blasted loudly from the Taj Cinema nearby and men and women lingered around the area, waiting for movie screenings. The barracks where Adi's family now lived was, the Indian landlord told them, fully occupied by Malay families. The entire barrack house was still fairly new. It had a zinc roof, and the walls of the building were still in satisfactory condition. The floor was a mix of cement and rough gravel, unlike the mud floor in Adi's old house. Their unit consisted of a room and a small veranda in the front. The small room could accommodate a single bed and a wardrobe, and the veranda could hold about six chairs and a table, to entertain guests. The kitchen was also located towards the front part of the house, with the bathroom in the rear, equipped with a shower. The latrines were located outside near the bathroom, two cubicles with three steps leading up to each of them.

• • •

The first night in his new home, Adi had difficulty falling asleep. He was restless, as was Mak Timah. Kak Habsah had just left after having a long chat with her. Adi was not used to staying in a house with electric lights. When the lights were switched off, Mak Timah asked Adi to light up the kerosene lamp. They were accustomed to its dim and faint light. Adi lay down on the veranda but could not sleep. The image of his banyan tree appeared in his mind. He imagined that he was climbing the tree and could see into its cavity. In his mind's eye, the leaves of the banyan tree gleamed softly in the moonlight. Adi was not sure at what time he finally dozed off, but in his dreams, he could smell the mud floor of his old house. The next day, Adi told his mother about his dream. Mak Timah said that it would, of course, be hard to completely forget something that one was so familiar with.

The next day, after school, Adi went back to his old house. He walked inside, looked at the ambin, his empty room, and the kitchen. He felt as though the walls reflected gloom and sadness and the mud floor wailed with his pain. He went to the bathroom. Its floor was dry. Adi stared at the walls, feeling despondent. He first sat and then lay down on the ambin for a while. He could hear the sounds from Ah Kong's Rediffusion. Adi moved over to the window and opened it. He looked out at the banyan tree. It no longer looked the same to his eyes; it seemed to have shrunk in the one day he'd been gone. He took one last look around his old house, and then cycled back to Jalan Turi.

Adi found it just as difficult to sleep for the next few nights as he had the first night in the new house. The image of the banyan tree kept recurring in his dreams. He kept having the feeling that he was touching the wall of the well. He smelt the mud floor of his old house. Mak Timah too had hardly slept since they had moved. Pungut alone slept soundly; she did not care whether she was in a new place or old. Everything was the same to her. Kak Habsah also had difficulty falling asleep. She kept thinking of her old house and of Abang Dolah.

• • •

After about a week of living in the barrack house, Adi began to get acquainted with his neighbours. The neighbour to their right was a policeman, and he had three children. Next to the policeman lived a taxi driver from Malacca, and to his right was a hawker who sold mee rebus at Queen Cinema. Whenever the hawker came back from work, there would be a tricycle parked in front of his unit. Adi did not know yet who lived next to Kak Habsah's unit, though he often saw two young girls doing their laundry at the end of the barracks on that side.

The scene in front of Jalan Turi, which was not far from the Taj Cinema, was always a very busy one. In the evenings, many people did their shopping at Geylang Serai. Adi had yet to go out and mix with the other Malay children of the area; they were always hanging around a big boulder that was on the side of a street junction until late at night. Adi had not made any new friends since he had moved to Jalan Turi. He spent most of his time at school. When he was done with school, he would drop by his old house before going home. He began reading even more books since his move to Jalan Turi. The smell of the mud floor of his old house seemed to beckon him to return there. He imagined that he kept hearing Ah Kong's Rediffusion night after night as he struggled to sleep.

ABANG DOLAH FREED

NO ONE IN the world was happier that day than Kak Habsah. It was a beautiful evening. This sweet Hari Raya was one she would never forget. How could she, when all of a sudden the one person whom she had been waiting for appeared unexpectedly at her door. Abang Dolah had been set free, even though there had been no prior indication that he would be released. Kak Habsah cried as she embraced her bone-thin lover. His face was pale and he looked haggard. Abang Dolah and Kak Habsah hugged each other for a long while. He then shifted his attention to Adi and hugged him as well.

"You've grown up. At what level are you now?" he asked, in his usual friendly manner. Mak Timah also burst into tears at the joyful sight. "I feel liberated, all praises to Allah," he said. That evening, Abang Dolah related his experiences in jail until late into the night. "Nothing is more precious in this world than freedom," he declared.

The next morning Abang Dolah invited Adi to accompany him as he went to look for his old friends at Kampung Pak Buyung. They found that only Daud Cina was still living there; the rest had relocated to other parts of Singapore. Abang Dolah also invited Adi to take a look at his old room. Thereafter the two of them stopped by

Bibik's house to chat.

"Don't mix with bad company anymore," advised Bibik. Abang Dolah laughed. He then listened as Adi told him a lengthy story about the recent riots.

That evening they returned to Jalan Turi. Abang Dolah planned to hold a wedding feast the next month, to celebrate his marriage to Kak Habsah.

Adi noticed a big change in Abang Dolah's behaviour. He now never missed his prayers. After the call to prayer was recited each of its six times during the day, Abang Dolah would kneel and say his praises to Allah for a long time. He would then read from the Quran. Adi supposed that life in prison had brought Abang Dolah closer to Allah.

Kak Habsah was most happy to see Abang Dolah's reformation. She invited Adi to go with her to the Habib Noh Shrine at Tanjong Pagar, to offer bananas and yellow rice there. "To fulfil my vow," she explained.

Adi had found his friend again. He now had someone to refer to when in doubt and to seek advice. Abang Dolah was trying to set up a business; he wanted to open a stall selling banana fritters. Once he had the capital, he would start selling Malay kuih. In his free time, Abang Dolah would play his violin as before. He talked a lot about religion, and intended to run classes in his house on reciting the Quran. "To gain spiritual points," explained Abang Dolah with a wink.

PART

3

CONFRONTATION

ADI RUSHED HOME. "There's been an explosion! There's been an explosion! Someone's set off a bomb!" Adi was breathing hard as he conveyed the news that he had heard over the radio. A bomb had gone off at the Hong Kong & Shanghai Bank at Orchard Road.

"Some Indonesians planted a bomb! People are dead!" Kak Habsah in turn relayed the news. "Don't go outdoors, there are bombs!"

Mak Timah was shocked to hear the news. She stopped in the middle of feeding Pungut, who shook her head as she waited for her meal to continue. "Are many people dead?"

"I don't know, but some people have died!" Kak Habsah replied.

"Who bombed?" Mak Timah wondered aloud, her eyes wide and unblinking.

"Indonesians, the Indonesians!"

That night Abang Dolah relayed the news that Soekarno had declared a Konfrontasi against Malaysia and that Indonesia had withdrawn from the United Nations. "We must be vigilant. Don't walk freely in unfamiliar places. It's dangerous!"

"Don't you go roaming about," Mak Timah said to Adi.

"Just now, Dolah Supik asked me to go look at the

scene of the explosion. I was scared to go, so he went alone," Adi replied.

"Soekarno wants to crush Malaysia," said Abang Dolah. "No one expected him to launch an open attack. What misfortune has befallen us! Ours will be a bloody history. Killing one's own kin. Killing each other. Those who died were innocent. This is all the fault of the Communists. Soekarno must have been taken in by their evil talk. How heartless of him to shed the blood of his own race! What fate has befallen us!"

"Why does Indonesia hate Malaysia?" Kak Habsah asked earnestly.

"Yes, why must they bomb our country? Why kill innocent people?" interjected Mak Timah.

"Even if I tried to explain, neither of you would understand. This is politics! Politics! It's hard to explain," Abang Dolah replied.

"Yes, but why kill others? Curse the culprits! So heartless! Why kill the innocent?" Kak Habsah continued to wonder.

"If they want war, then fight a *real* war. Soldiers against soldiers. Why must they bomb Orchard Road? There were no soldiers there," added Mak Timah.

Abang Dolah remained silent. He was in no mood to answer their questions. He found it difficult to explain Soekarno's political schemes to both of them.

Mak Timah turned to Adi again. "You better don't wander," she said. "After school, just stay at home and don't roam about for no reason. Who knows, there might be more bombs elsewhere!"

Adi's attention was on Abang Dolah. "Soekarno wants to attack our country, is it? If Indonesia attacks us, how? Can we fight back?" he asked.

"I don't think they want to attack our country, they only want to scare us. They just want to threaten us so that the ideal of Malaysia will be abandoned," Abang Dolah explained.

He frowned. If Indonesia had been invited to join Malaysia, surely such a tragedy would not have come to pass. If only Indonesia had been consulted, had been asked to join the union just as the goat's head party had suggested in their manifesto, surely Soekarno would not have launched his attack. In this instance, Abang Dolah felt that the goat's head party had shown much more foresight than the other political parties.

He took off his glasses. Without his spectacles, Abang Dolah's eyes seemed perceptibly sunken. Two impressions had been left on either side of his nose.

"Soekarno may have felt that Indonesia has been marginalised, ostracised, its opinions disregarded. Maybe that's why he is upset," he added.

"If they want to fight, then fight properly!" Mak Timah said, taking up the refrain yet again. "Instead they bombed a civilian place, many innocent people died! What is this?"

• • •

As the days passed, the Indonesian attacks escalated. More public places were bombed. The car park at Odeon Cinema was bombed. The Hotel Ambassador at Katong Park was bombed. A public telephone booth at Jalan Rebong was bombed. An Indian shopkeeper died when a bomb exploded in a back lane off MacPherson Road. Public panic mounted. No one dared to go out to work. School students were terrified. Everyone was afraid that a bomb might go off at any time. The people stirred themselves into a frenzy talking about how the bombs were all over the place. It was all everyone could think about. People became wary of unattended items. They dared not tinker with anything they came across. Students were told not to open any stray packages they found. Everyone was afraid. The lives of civilians were in danger. A bomb could go off anytime, anywhere. At any moment, lives could be lost. At any instant, limbs could be torn away, faces could be disfigured, and stomachs ripped open.

Mak Timah forbade Adi from going out after he came home from school, and she would give him a long lecture if he were late. He felt like a prisoner, just like during the riots in Kampung Pak Buyung. His mother forbade him from washing cars on Friday and Saturday nights, and from going out to look for scrap aluminium. Mak Timah herself was very careful whenever she went out to do laundry or go to Lorong 15 to give massages to women in confinement.

The Confrontation became more intense. Several Indonesian soldiers landed in Kota Tinggi and in Pasir Panjang. News of the arrest of armed soldiers was splashed across the newspapers, and the armed incursion was constantly mentioned on the radio.

"Two Indonesian soldiers are to be hanged tomorrow," Abang Dolah said one night, with a deep puff of his cigarette. "If they're hanged, there will be chaos; we don't know what could happen. Soekarno has said that he'll attack before the roosters crow."

That night, everyone stayed awake. The atmosphere at the barrack house was like that of Hari Raya, except with the absence of celebration in the air. Every house remained brightly lit until dawn. Adi did not sleep at all, and waited for the roosters to crow. But by dawn, Indonesia had not launched any attack.

The Indonesian soldiers were hanged as planned. Indonesia still did not attack, but everyone remained anxious. Adi's freedom continued to be curtailed; Mak Timah would nag him whenever he came back late from school, sometimes for a solid two hours. He was tired of listening to her griping, and he could not understand why such things had happened. During the Japanese invasion, bombs had fallen from the sky and people could run for cover. Now, they exploded in the middle of the road, or in the fields while people were playing soccer.

People began to imagine what would happen if Indonesia really invaded. Throughout the Confrontation, youngsters bandied about Soekarno's slogan "Ganyang Malaysia"—"Crush Malaysia". Eventually the bomb blasts subsided, but people remained suspicious and wary. Parents were still worried for their children's safety. Mak Timah, however, started to gradually give Adi back his freedom. He began to wash cars again on Friday and Saturday nights.

Ani came often to visit Mak Timah at Jalan Turi. Her daughter, Adi's niece, had grown playful and clever and could now respond to teasing. She could also understand if someone offered to buy her ice cream or sweets. But Ani's latest visit angered Mak Timah.

"Pungut should be sent to a welfare home," Ani said. "Of what use is looking after a retarded child like Pungut? It's pointless!"

Mak Timah lost her temper. "You're not the one looking after her; she doesn't depend on you!"

After that, Ani dared not to bring up the idea of sending Pungut away again. Mak Timah continued to mumble to herself even after Ani had gone home.

• • •

Adi now had even more subjects in school. There was much homework to be completed. He had to draw maps for geography, write English and Malay compositions, and solve mathematical problems. He struggled to complete his homework under the dim light of his kerosene lamp, making his eyes watery. He was most unenthusiastic about drawing; he only had stubby colour pencils. Often when he had to draw something, Adi would go to Salleh's house on Lorong 21 to borrow his art materials. When Salleh noticed how Adi struggled to draw, or could not stand seeing how ugly and messy Adi's work was, he would draw for him instead. The next day Adi would happily submit "his" drawing. One of these drawings was given high marks, and was also hung on the classroom wall. Adi smiled as he looked at his drawing, but then Salleh reminded him not to take credit for someone else's efforts.

The Confrontation was still on everyone's minds. People were still trying to predict when Indonesia would attack Malaysia. Indonesian paratroopers who landed at Labis and Kota Tinggi had been arrested. Many Malay soldiers had been killed. There were several arrests at Pasir Panjang, where more Indonesian soldiers had landed. The weapons seized during these arrests were kept on display in Community Centres, and the government encouraged people to go look at them. Adi had once gone with Abang Dolah to see the confiscated weapons: hand grenades, rifles, machine guns, bullets and Indonesian army uniforms. He had felt frightened.

"This conflict won't be for long; trust me, it will end soon," Abang Dolah reassured Adi. "Blood is thicker than water, trust me! Relatives will reunite when the rabble-rousers have gone away!"

Adi did not quite understand Abang Dolah's veiled

words. Although he had come across the proverb before, its meaning was still vague to him.

"This has all been instigated by the Communists! This is all their evil work!" Abang Dolah earnestly declared. "When the Indonesians realise they've been manipulated by the Communists, they will boycott the Confrontation with Malaysia! Trust me! Soekarno is trying to divert his people's attention by attacking Malaysia so that they will forget their own domestic problems! They are suffering in poverty! They are getting by only on corn! Soekarno is inciting his people on purpose. Malaysia is not a threat to Indonesia. Soon the Indonesians will wise up to Soekarno's political games. Trust me, you'll see. How long can Soekarno go on pulling the wool over his people's eyes? It's better for them to provide food for their hungry citizens than to buy weapons to fight Malaysia!

"This is a Communist strategy to destroy us; this is how they want to pit us against each other, even though we are of the same race and religion. I wonder how the Indonesians could have fallen for Soekarno's ploy. Where is their faith? Where is their pan-Malay spirit? They are so easily manipulated! So easily bought by the enemy!" Abang Dolah went on, though he seemed to be talking to himself.

Adi listened without a word. He could only pray that no more bombs would go off. If everything was peaceful, his mother would not worry about letting him walk along Aljunied Road to school. Adi only wanted to live free, as he had in the past. He wished for the freedom to bathe at Alkaff Garden, to walk along Kallang Puding searching for aluminium, to cut down coconut trees with Nordin Pendek in Siglap, Bedok, and Frankel Estate. It was all Adi wished for.

THE LAMP GROWS DIM

ABANG DOLAH FELL seriously ill. According to his doctor, he had stomach cancer. Kak Habsah cried over and over until her eyes were swollen. Abang Dolah's condition deteriorated quickly, and he became so weak that he could not get up out of bed. His body grew skeletal; he complained of stomachaches and groaned in pain day and night. Kak Habsah wanted to take him to the hospital but he declined.

"Let me die at home," Abang Dolah pleaded. Kak Habsah faithfully looked after him. He had started to defecate and urinate in his bed. As he could only lie on the bed all the time, his rear end grew sores and started to swell up. When Kak Habsah showed the sight to Adi, he was horrified. He felt sad to see Abang Dolah in pain all day and night.

Abang Dolah was no longer chatty. He only lay staring at the zinc roof above. He would whisper his prayers and call out praises to Allah, for the strength to endure his pain. The sores on his backside got worse, and Kak Habsah was forced to clean them every day. Abang Dolah was clearly going through great suffering. Whenever Adi visited, Abang Dolah could only squint at him. However, Kak Habsah was grateful that she was now married to Abang Dolah.

"I'm thankful that Allah has united me with Abang Dolah before he returns to Him. Even if he passes away, I won't have regrets," said Kak Habsah to Mak Timah.

Mak Timah helped to take care of Abang Dolah as best as she could. Adi would regularly buy cotton wool from the village shop for Mak Timah to use when she wiped Abang Dolah's body with warm water. Abang Dolah's condition worsened. The mattress he lay on was always moist and stained with his urine and faeces. The sores on his backside were spreading. He groaned throughout the day and night as he fought his illness. Adi felt heartbroken when he heard Abang Dolah moaning in pain. He no longer dared to look at Abang Dolah's festering rear end, nor did Mak Timah dare look at the rotting, smelly wound. Kak Habsah alone dared to clean Abang Dolah's backside. She would use a pair of pincers and cotton wool to clean the now-gaping sores, which, she told them, had developed pus. Kak Habsah had become visibly thinner. Her face looked bony and she no longer bothered to dress up. Her already-faded sarong and baju kurung looked perpetually soiled, her hair remained dishevelled, and she no longer put on make-up and mascara.

Amid this sad atmosphere, the Confrontation with Indonesia continued. Soekarno talked incessantly about destroying Malaysia. While incidents of bomb blasts had become rare, the atmosphere remained tense. The people had not forgotten the bloody bomb blasts at the Hong Kong & Shanghai Bank at Orchard Road, the telephone booth at Jalan Rebong, and the Ambassador Hotel at Katong Park. As long as the Confrontation was on, the fear would remain. Soekarno kept crying "Crush Malaysia!" and the conflict would continue for another year.

• • •

Abang Dolah's condition continued to degenerate. He passed out several times a day and could only speak a few words at a time. Nevertheless, he would squint at Adi, and try to smile. For his part, Adi would hold Abang Dolah's limp hand in his. The veins on Abang Dolah's arms appeared greenish and criss-crossed. His skin was sagging and pale. Adi could not bear to visit Abang Dolah anymore because whenever he saw him, he was reduced to tears.

Meanwhile, the position of Singapore's state within Malaysia had become the subject of much contention and debate. There were many problems, and political relations with Kuala Lumpur grew very tense.

Kak Habsah was forced to quit her job in order to take care of Abang Dolah. Of late, he had been groaning less loudly. Kak Habsah still wanted to take him to the hospital, but whenever she raised the topic with Abang Dolah, he would shake his head and whisper, "Let me die at home. Let me die...in your lap." After that, Kak Habsah did not have the heart to send Abang Dolah to the hospital.

The lamp in Kak Habsah's room was growing dimmer one evening. A number of flying ants buzzed around the bulb. There was a skinny lizard with a long tail on the wall right next to the display cabinet. Kak Habsah was boiling some water to wipe Abang Dolah's now-scrawny body. Abang Dolah's eyes had sunk deeper into their sockets, but his shrunken eyelids made his eyes protrude further still. His lips were always dry and his pained groans would touch anyone who heard the sound.

Adi took Abang Dolah's hands in his. Abang Dolah stared at him for a long time. He then began to speak, very softly. Adi brought his head close to Abang Dolah's lips to hear him whisper: "I'm going to die, Adi. When I'm dead, you may have all my books."

Adi squeezed Abang Dolah's hands tight and nodded. He then looked away, staring at the small, dim light bulb. Kak Habsah entered with a basin and towel to wash Abang Dolah. Adi went out.

• • •

Members of the flame logo party had challenged members of the axe logo party to debate. Immigrants too raised debates on the rights given to the bumiputeras, the "indigenous people". The sovereignty of the sultans had come into question and some people had begun to boldly demand the abolition of special rights for the bumiputeras. The slogan "Malaysian Malaysia" echoed more often. The people were confused. The flame logo party—the ruling party in the state of Singapore—asked for more rights from Kuala Lumpur, and there were many altercations as a result. Challenges and counter-challenges were bandied about, and blame was thrown back and forth. Relations between Kuala Lumpur and Singapore became palpably strained. Something bad was going to happen. Like the cancer in Abang Dolah's stomach, it was waiting to erupt.

SEPARATION

ABANG DOLAH HAD been calm since morning. He no longer cried out in pain. Kak Habsah had called a doctor, who had given Abang Dolah an injection to ease his pain. His condition appeared to have improved slightly, but only just.

Adi was shocked to hear the news broadcast over the radio. Thunder seemed to rumble through his ears. He felt as if a heavy mountain pressed down on his chest. Tears welled up in his eyes.

"Singapore has separated from Malaysia!" the newscaster announced.

In a whisper, he conveyed the news to Abang Dolah. His old friend's eyes glistened in their sockets. He whispered back softly to Adi, his speech laboured and his words drawn out. "Betrayed...future...bleak. You have... no...future!"

Adi held Abang Dolah's hand in a firm grip.

Tears rolled down his cheeks.

ACKNOWLEDGEMENTS

A work of fiction would not be fiction if it had not been for the commitment of the characters that manipulate the plot to reach its climax. Confrontation reaches its climax because of the contributions of history and the environment I was born into. This environment I vividly resurrect for the benefit of readers to experience the true facet of humanity in confronting life's most challenging moments.

On the same note, readers would not have been confronted with *Confrontation* if it had not been for the following individuals and organisations: Mohamed Pitchay Gani Mohamed Abdul Aziz, for his initiatives and ongoing commitment towards this publication; the National Arts Council, for their generous support in terms of translation and publication grants; Angkatan Sasterawan '50, for embarking on the translation of the Malay version of this novel into English, and applying for the NAC grant; Muhammad Herwanto Johari, for his inputs and proofreading, Dr Krishna Udayasankar for initially line editing the translated manuscript; Edmund Wee, for his expert advice and for publishing this book; and finally Jason Erik Lundberg, for his personal touches and creativity on editing this book, and also (most importantly) for coming up with the title that very much expresses my confrontation with reality. To all, please accept my most humble gratitude.

ABOUT THE AUTHOR

MOHAMED LATIFF MOHAMED is one of the most prolific writers to come after the first generation of writers in the Singapore Malay literary scene. His many accolades include the Montblanc-NUS Centre for the Arts Literary Award (1998), the SEA Write Award (2002), the Tun Seri Lanang Award (Malay Language Council of Singapore, Ministry of Information, Communication and the Arts) (2003), the National Arts Council Special Recognition Award (2009), and the Singapore Literature Prize in 2004, 2006 and 2008. His works revolve around the life and struggles of the Malay community in pre- and post-independence Singapore, and have been translated into Chinese, English, German and Korean.

The original Malay edition of *Confrontation*, titled *Batas Langit*, was awarded Consolation Prize in 1999 for the Malay Literary Award organised by the Malay Language Council of Singapore, and selected in 2005 for the READ! Singapore nationwide reading initiative organised by the National Library Board.

ABOUT THE TRANSLATOR

SHAFFIQ SELAMAT (widely known in the Malay literature world as Shasel) is the author of short story collection *Meredah Badai* (*Braving the Storm*, 2005), and the translator of two novels: *Aylana* by Manaf Hamzah (2012) and *Confrontation* by Mohamed Latiff Mohamed (2013). He started writing in the early 1990s by joining the Teens Writing Club of *Berita Harian* (KCR-BH), while working as a translator at Singapore's Ministry of Foreign Affairs. His poems, essays and short stories (in both Malay and English) have been published in *Berita Harian*, *Berita Minggu* and *Manik-manik Hijau* (*Green Beads*), in addition to other literary anthologies and entertainment and educational magazines. His poem "Bicara Keemasan (Golden Conversation)" won first runner-up in the Moving Words 2011 poetry competition.